A hard rain. Ha... streets and back... radiator behind... valiant fight to k... Beyond the sing... far-off ship's horn echoed through the fog and rain, crying out like a lost animal in the night.

I loved the city, every stinking thing about it.

I nestled my fedora down tight on my head and pulled the collar of my coat up around my neck as I glanced one more time around my office. The single wood desk commanded the room. The empty chair behind the desk sat with its back to the city beyond the window, as if what went on out there on those damp streets meant nothing.

But that wasn't true.

The city was like a dame, demanding attention, taking what it could and giving back even more. But for the moment, it would have to wait. I had just finished one case. I wanted to savor the feeling of putting the creep behind bars, where he belonged.

With one last glance at the cars splashing water on the black streets below my window, I turned and said, "Computer. Door."

Then with a few steps I left room 312, my office, the office of Dixon Hill, Private Investigator, and strolled onto the perfectly lit, comfortably warm corridors of the *Enterprise*.

Little did I know that I would be forced to return to those cold, wet streets of 1941 San Francisco much sooner than planned. And for a reason much more deadly than any simple Dixon Hill murder case. . . .

STAR TREK
THE NEXT GENERATION®

A HARD RAIN

Dean Wesley Smith

Based upon STAR TREK and
STAR TREK: THE NEXT GENERATION
created by Gene Roddenberry

POCKET BOOKS
New York   London   Toronto   Sydney   Singapore

This book is a work of fiction. Names, characters, places and incidents are products of the author's imagination or are used fictitiously. Any resemblance to actual events or locales or persons, living or dead, is entirely coincidental.

An *Original* Publication of POCKET BOOKS

POCKET BOOKS, a division of Simon & Schuster, Inc.
1230 Avenue of the Americas, New York, NY 10020

This book is published by Pocket Books, a division of
Simon & Schuster, Inc., under exclusive license from
Paramount Pictures.

ISBN: 0-7434-1926-X

First Pocket Books printing March 2002

10 9 8 7 6 5 4 3 2 1

POCKET and colophon are registered trademarks of
Simon & Schuster, Inc.

For information regarding special discounts for bulk purchases, please
contact Simon & Schuster Special Sales at 1-800-456-6798 or
business@simonandschuster.com

Printed in the U.S.A.

For the wonderful mystery writer, Kris Nelscott.
Dixon Hill and I thank you.

A HARD RAIN

Chapter One

A Hardboiled Life in the City

Section One: On the Hunt

IT WAS RAINING IN THE CITY by the bay. A hard rain. Hard enough to wash the slime out of the streets.

Dixon Hill thought back over the words of his friend, Mr. Data, as the radiator behind him cracked and popped. It fought the valiant battle to keep the cold and damp out of his office. It usually lost.

Beyond the single pane window the deep sounds of a far-off ship's horn echoed through the fog and rain, crying out like a lost animal in the night.

He listened. Many days he had just sat, feet up on his desk, and listened to that deep, mournful sound. Now it faded, replaced by the honking of cars and swishing of tires on the wet pavement of the street below. He loved the city, every rotten, lustful, dark thing about it.

But right now he wished he could make the whole stinking place just go away.

Dixon Hill sighed and listened as the ship's horn again moaned its plaintive cry. So far he had been lucky in this world. He doubted his luck was going to hold.

He nestled his gray fedora tight on his head, straightened his tie, and pulled the collar of his tan raincoat up around his neck. Then he touched the scarred top of the single wood desk that commanded the room. The empty, wooden chair behind the desk sat with its back to the city, seeming to say that nothing out there meant anything.

But that wasn't true.

The city demanded attention, taking what it could like a hungry beast always searching for food. He had still not finished one case, had not managed to put the creep who had killed Marci Andrews behind bars where he belonged. She had been a great actress, and was gunned down at her stage door, and Dixon Hill had wanted to find her killer.

He had not done so, and that bothered him.

But now he had to get to work on something far more important. He had to find the Heart of the Adjuster. The Adjuster itself was a device not much bigger than a loaf of bread. The Heart of the Adjuster was what made it important. The Heart, a small, golden ball that rattled around inside the Adjuster, was what made the thing work. Without it, like a human without a heart pumping blood, the Adjuster was worthless.

Now the Heart of the Adjuster had been snatched without anyone leaving so much as a clue. But Dixon Hill knew that with any crime, there were always clues. You just had to know where to look.

And Dixon Hill was a master of turning over every rock and finding those clues.

He moved so that his nose was close to the cold glass of the wet window. Out there somewhere, hidden in the large city, was the Heart of the Adjuster. But where?

Hill's breath fogged the window, reminding him that he was still alive, for the moment. The stakes of this heist were even higher than a simple murder case. This time the lives of hundreds rested with his ability to dig out what had happened to the Heart of the Adjuster, shovelful by shovelful, until he had moved enough dirt to expose the worms that lived in the dirt and grime of this city. Only then would he find who had taken the Heart, where it was hidden, and end all this.

No one stood below, on the sidewalk, in the rain, waiting for him.

Good. It was time to go.

He made sure his notebook was in his pocket, then turned and headed for the door.

Granted, he had his doubts about his ability, more so this time than any case ever before. He hoped he was as good as everyone said he was. Because if he wasn't, the price was going to be high. Failure this time meant the wet streets of San Francisco would swallow him like so much garbage, taking the hundreds of others who depended on him down as well. For without the Heart, nothing would last long.

Once before this world had endangered everything, in his very first venture here, when he was working a case he called, "The Big Good-bye." But this time it wasn't just some alliance that was at stake. It was lives.

His and everyone else's.

He had to be Dixon Hill, the best P.I. in the city by the bay, to solve this case. He would do that.

And be that.

He had no choice.

He closed the door to his inner office hard, like a period on a short sentence, closing off the doubts. Then he headed through his outer office toward the stairs, squaring his shoulders to meet the city, pushing the last shreds of questions to the bottom of his mind as if trying to drown them in a shallow pool. He would have to hold those doubts under, kill them without remorse. Weakness was never an option on the streets of this city.

A cat streaked down the hall and out of sight around the corner, silent and alone in its dealings. He felt that way as well. Alone, stalking his prey through this man-made jungle.

He closed the outer door, rattling the glass with his name etched on it.

Then, without a glance back, he went down the stairs.

Dixon Hill was on the case.

*Thirty-one hours before
the Heart of the Adjuster is stolen*

Captain's Log. Personal.

*My hope is that with more than eight hours
remaining before the* Enterprise *reaches the area
nicknamed the* Blackness, *I will have the time to solve
the fascinating Dixon Hill case I have nicknamed
"Murder at the Stage Door." If I succeed, it will be the
tenth Dixon Hill case I will have solved since my first
visit to this strange holographic world. And I am proud
to say that each case has been progressively harder
than the one before it. Dr. Crusher tells me the
challenge and the change of scenery improve my mood
and efficiency and I am in no position to argue with
her. After all, she is the ship's doctor.*

*Nevertheless, the challenge is engrossing. And the
change of reality, from my shipboard duties to being a
private detective in old San Francisco, is attractive to
me. Being able to change reality so simply is a luxury I
have not taken for granted.*

*I, as Dixon Hill, have only two real suspects in the
death of actress Marci Andrews. The first, her husband,
producer Arnie Andrews, seems the most likely
candidate. The second, her spurned lover, Brad
Barringer, seems far more upset than he should,
considering the circumstances.*

*On the surface, the case seems so simple: jealous
husband, tossed-aside boyfriend. Yet my instincts tell me
that Cyrus Redblock, crime boss of the city, is involved. I*

just haven't made the connection yet. But in the next eight hours I hope to do just that.

Section Two: A Friendly Greeting

Dixon Hill listened to his own footsteps echoing between the dark buildings.

Click. Click. Click.

The hard heels of his dress shoes made the wet pavement ring like a drummer keeping perfect time. He made no effort to silence the beat. For the moment the rain had stopped, leaving the city black and shiny under the streetlights, yet at the same time pitch dark and forbidding between each island of light.

In perfect time he moved from darkness to light, then back to darkness, never slowing.

A swirling fog drifted just overhead, threatening to lower a blanket of gray onto the street at any moment. The air smelled of dampness and fish from the docks. Again he pulled his collar up against his neck, trying to get it tighter to hold out the air's thick, heavy feel. It felt like a force that he had to push through.

Click. Click. Click.

The cadence of his shoes echoed so loud in the narrow, building-lined street that he knew no one was following him. He would be able to hear them like a drum corps marching in a parade.

He reached a major street corner and turned onto a bright active area, lit like a stage by the yellow lights in the windows and signs flashing with garish colors.

He paused for a moment before stepping onto that stage, then pushed the doubts away and moved into the light.

Cars sped past, the sounds of their engines filling the background of the place like thunder from a distant storm. No one paid him any attention, as he hoped would be the case. His own steps were lost in the music of the night and the performances going on around him.

Late theater patrons, mostly couples arm in arm, hurried past him, heading for their cars, the streetcars, or maybe a nearby after-show dinner.

He watched them, wishing for the freedom they enjoyed. He and the elegant Bev had taken in a show along with dinner one night just a month before, leaving Mr. Data to guard a warehouse while waiting for the arrival of Cyrus Redblock.

As they often did, Mr. Data and Bev had been helping him work a case he called "Murder under the Bridge." He had solved it in three days' time. Easy as pie, as Mr. Data would say. After that one night on the town, word had got around that she was his steady squeeze. He let it spread. He could do worse.

The image of the Luscious Bev that night flashed back to him. Her tight red dress, her hair long and full, her lips painted red. He had never remembered her being so beautiful. Yes, he could do worse. A whole lot worse.

Some night he planned on taking up his friend, Detective Bell, on his offer to bring the Luscious Bev over to meet his wife and kids. If he, and the rest of this world, survived this case, he would do just that. He'd been wanting to meet that wife Bell kept bragging about.

Now, the Luscious Bev, Mr. Whelan, Mr. Data, and a number of others were helping him on this case. He had a hunch they were not going to be the only ones.

Dix pushed the image away and focused on the task at hand. He knew that finding the Heart of the Adjuster was going to take all of his people, especially if they were going to find it in time to save this city. And everyone beyond the confines of this wet, dark world.

Ahead, three parked cars away, a man stood, his back against a light pole, his jacket open like he welcomed the wetness. The burning ember on the end of a cigarette hung like a beacon, orange against the black shadows.

Dix studied him like an art collector studying an interesting painting. The guy had been waiting long enough to burn through five cigs, the butts pressed into the wet pavement around him.

The man pretended to pay no attention to anything, as if he were only waiting for time to pass.

Dix almost laughed. He knew the guy had seen him by the slight jerk of his head, and by the way he did everything in his power not to look in Dix's direction.

It was Dix he had been waiting for.

But for what reason? That was going to be the big

money question. Maybe right now, right here, Dix was going to get his first clue as to who took the Heart.

Dix didn't recognize the guy's mug, but the way the city and the world around Dixon Hill had changed over the last number of hours, that didn't mean anything. The guy was good-sized, with bulges in all the wrong places under the brown raincoat. It was easy to see the guy's guns by how he leaned against the pole, pulling his coat tight against them.

The guy was stupid. Dumber than the streetlight he was leaning against. Or maybe that saying was *nowhere near as bright?* Dix sometimes confused the sayings of the day. Mr. Data and the Luscious Bev were always correcting him.

Dix didn't vary his pace.

As he got within a step of passing the man's position, the guy reached into his coat to pull his gun from the holster bulging under his arm.

Real slow and real stupid.

The guy didn't get the piece clear of his armpit.

Dix spun, stepped toward the guy, and put his fist squarely against the side of the guy's jaw, swinging through as if trying to hit a spot just out of reach beyond the weak chin.

The big lug became as loose as a rag doll, spinning around the pole and landing facedown on the hood of a blue Dodge with a loud thump, denting the metal. The guy's big gun clattered on the sidewalk and ended up in the water in the gutter.

Dix flipped the bag of flesh over, then grabbed him

by the front of his shirt and coat and hauled him up close. The guy's gray eyes read dumb, and his legs were playing at good imitations of wet noodles.

But stupid boy wasn't done being stupid yet. Stunned, he still had enough left to try to struggle.

Real bad thinking.

Dix pounded him hard in the stomach, his fist sinking into the soft flesh just above his belt.

The guy doubled over with a choking sound, like a cat trying to cough up a fur ball. Dix stepped sideways to make sure nothing from the guy's dinner ended up on his shoes.

It took a moment, then the guy caught his breath as if coming up from trying to swim a lap of the YMCA pool under water.

A couple moved to the inside of the sidewalk to avoid the scene, keeping their heads down and walking past quickly. Smart folks, keeping their noses clean.

Dix grabbed the guy's lapel again and hauled him back to a standing position. For a second time Dix brought him up close, staring into the gray eyes.

"You want to tell me why you were about to pull a gun on me?" Dix asked, his voice as low and as cold as he could make it, his nose just inches from the other man's nose. "Spill it."

Dix could tell the guy was going to have a sore jaw for a week. He moved it before speaking and the smell of garlic filled Dix's face like the air blowing from an Italian restaurant exhaust fan. Dix held his grip and his ground and kept staring into the man's dull eyes.

"Orders," the guy said, finally, wincing at the pain as he spoke. "I'm supposed ta put ya on ice and bring ya ta my boss."

Even through the Italian-rot breath, Dix knew the guy was telling the truth. The eyes didn't move, the body didn't jerk.

"And who is your boss?" Dix demanded, not allowing himself to blink.

The guy's eyes shifted right, then left, making sure no one was listening. "Benny da Banger," the guy said, the garlic adding intensity to the words.

Dix shoved the guy hard against the hood of the car, denting it again. He was clearly too stupid to be lying. He really did work for someone named Benny the Banger.

Dix had never heard of anyone with that name.

"So what does this *Benny* want with me?"

"Benny wanted ta make sure ya stayed out'a his way when he takes over the city," the guy said, leaning against the Dodge while rubbing his jaw with the back of his hand.

Dix laughed. "I think Cyrus Redblock might have a problem with that idea."

The guy snorted. "Ya been on vacation or somethin'? Redblock's out of the picture. Someone snatched him. City's up for grabs and my boss wants a part of it."

Dix kept his face calm and straight, not letting it show the surprise he felt. If Redblock was gone, that meant finding the Heart of the Adjuster was going to be that much harder. And that much more dangerous.

"I'm cuttin' ya loose," Dix said. "Tell your boss I won't get in his way if he doesn't get in mine."

Still rubbing his jaw, the guy nodded.

Dix turned and headed down the dark, wet street toward where he was to meet the Luscious Bev and Mr. Data on their stakeout.

Behind him he could hear a soft cussing sound as Benny's goon picked his gun from the dirty water and held it up like a day old fish. Swimmin' in the gutter couldn't be good on a piece.

Twenty-seven hours before
the Heart of the Adjuster is heisted

Captain's Log. Personal.
The Enterprise *is still four hours from the* Blackness *and none of the crew seems to have any more information about what it is than they did four hours ago. It seems we have a major mystery facing us.*

As Dr. Crusher has ordered for my mental health, I spent the hours relaxing on the holodeck as Dixon Hill. I have just returned from a very interesting chat with Cyrus Redblock, the crime boss of the city. He had paced in his plush office on the second floor of a warehouse, his coat off, his hat on the hat rack, his face red from the movement of his solid frame back and forth. He had told me, in no uncertain terms, that he had nothing to do with the murder of the actress Marci Andrews. And he didn't know who did.

Period. End of story, is exactly what he said.

But he let slip one important detail. Just as I had enjoyed Mrs. Andrew's shows, so had he. I have the gut feeling, from his comments, that he had cared for her more than as just a member of her audience.

But if that is the case, I have even less reason to suspect that he was involved with her death.

The case of "Murder at the Stage Door" is turning out to be a fascinating case that may take until after our exploration of the Blackness *to solve.*

One mystery at a time.

Section Three: War Ain't Pretty

The fog rolled in like an unwanted visitor demanding to be noticed. Dixon Hill turned off the brighter main thoroughfare onto a dark and narrow side street. The gray mist closed in around him, making the nearest building seem impossibly distant. It was as if he'd stepped into another world.

He felt alone.

The swirling fog blocked even the traffic sounds behind him. One streetlight fought against the black shadows and lost.

He kept moving, not letting his pace change. His steps now sounded like they were coming from someone else a long distance away. His face was wet from the mist, and the smell of the fish houses on the docks clogged his nose.

He couldn't see it, but he knew that ahead on his right was a warehouse that up until a few minutes ago he thought had housed Cyrus Redblock's gang. Dix had been in the plush office on the second floor of that warehouse a number of times, the most recent while working on the murder of the actress.

After the Heart of the Adjuster had been taken, Dix had ordered Mr. Data, Mr. Whelan, and two others to go to a location across from this warehouse to watch and wait. Bev had joined them with even more help a short time later.

But if Redblock had been snatched, as the goon working for Benny the Banger had claimed, it was going to throw a monkey wrench into all of Dix's plans. And they didn't have much time for too many delays.

A shape appeared out of the fog just in front of Dix, drifting through the mist as if his feet didn't touch the ground. The man's white hat and pale skin seemed to glow in the faint light as he moved silently forward.

"Sir," Mr. Data said, "No one has left or entered the building."

"Thank you," Dix said. "And Mr. Data, address me as Dix, or Dixon Hill while we are in here. No sirs. Understand? No point in causing any confusion."

"Yes, s—, uhh, Dix."

"Get the others," Dix said. "We're going in."

Without a sound Mr. Data turned and vanished into the fog like a ghost moving through a wall.

Dix walked on down the street toward the side door of the warehouse, his heels doing a distant drum roll on the pavement, muffled, without an echo.

Normally one of Redblock's men would be outside

the door, leaning against the wall, smoking one cig after another. But as the door appeared through the fog, Dix could tell something was very wrong. There was no guard, and the door stood open, a black, yawning hole no doubt leading to more problems.

Dix paused and waited until Data and the others appeared out of the swirling mist, moving across the street toward him. Data and the Luscious Bev led the way, followed by Whelan, Carter, Stanley, and Douglas.

A small gang for the moment. Others were getting ready to join them. Dix hoped he wasn't going to need the help.

He had no doubt he was.

"I've been told that Redblock's been snatched," Dix said. "But let's not take any chances. Go in slow and easy."

"Snatched by who?" Bev asked, her voice low and sultry as she moved to stand beside him. She was as beautiful as ever, even with the moisture pushing her hair against her head under the wide brim of her hat.

"We find that out," Dix whispered, "I suspect we find what we are looking for."

"Ready, s—, uh, boss," Data said.

Dix nodded. "Mr. Data, go to the right, Mr. Stanley and Mr. Carter, you go left. Mr. Douglas and Mr. Whelan, you remain out here on guard. I don't want to be surprised in there."

Everyone nodded.

"Find some lights and get them on," Dix said. "And let's be careful. These bullets can kill us just as fast, and just as completely, as any weapon we've ever seen."

"Gotcha, boss," Data said. Then he hitched up his pants and stood in his gangster posture. "As Mack Bolen once said, 'I can only die one death at a time.'"

Dixon Hill just stared at his friend until finally Mr. Data nodded and stepped silently through the door, followed at once by Stanley and Carter, their guns drawn.

The mist swirled between Dix and Bev as they waited, mixing the sound of his own breathing with the silence of the narrow street. The fog so dampened the sound that it seemed impossible that they were standing in the middle of a major city.

Suddenly the yellow of a faint light framed the doorway, casting a square of light into the street.

Dix nodded to Whelan, then stepped through into the high-ceilinged warehouse.

And into a bloodbath.

The space was stacked with wooden crates, all sealed. A half dozen cars were scattered around, all pointed at the closed main door of the warehouse, as if poised for a quick getaway that clearly hadn't happened.

Dix recognized the cream and white of Redblock's car. The man never went anywhere in the city without that car. Yet there it sat.

Dix took his time as he studied the large room. Bodies were everywhere, scattered around like dolls thrown by an angry child. From the looks of them, all had been Redblock's men, gunned down in what appeared to be a very intense fight.

Bullets had torn up everything, including the side of Redblock's car. The place smelled of gunpowder and blood.

Too much blood.

Dix studied the scene, noting the details and where some of the men must have made a stand against a large force coming in from the back of the building. This hadn't happened that long ago. Maybe two to four hours at most.

Maybe right after someone had taken the Heart of the Adjuster.

Mr. Data stood in the doorway leading to a flight of stairs. Stanley had taken up a position to the right of the door behind a crate. Dix motioned that Stanley stay in position. "Carter, check out the back area."

"Oh, my," Bev said, moving toward one of the closest bodies. She bent over the man in a black suit, then turned to Dix and shook her head. "Looks like we're in a full war. Someone shot this man a few extra times to make sure he was dead."

In all the cases Dix had worked in this city, he had never seen or heard of such carnage. Clearly the reality of this city had changed.

No one was safe.

He had known that. The blood splattered everywhere, like a mad child had gotten into red paint, just put a very clear exclamation point on the sentence.

"Stay alert," Dix said.

He and Bev stepped over one twisted body and headed toward Mr. Data. He wasn't sure what they were going to find in Redblock's office, but they had to look.

And after that? What was next?

Dixon Hill had no idea. Somehow, they needed to find the Heart of the Adjuster and find it fast. But from the looks of what had happened to Redblock's men, that task had just gotten harder.

And far, far more dangerous.

*Twenty-five hours before
the Heart of the Adjuster is snatched*

Captain's Log. Personal.

The Enterprise *is two hours from the* Blackness *and still none of my crew can tell me exactly what is causing it. Mr. Data believes it may be an area of space influenced by a nearby quantum singularity, but we have studied thousands of black holes and none have caused this type of dampening of all sensors and twisting of light in such a large area. No one is even sure exactly where the effects start, only that light seems to vanish at a certain point ahead of us, and no sensors can get through that point.*

I have ordered the ship to approach slowly and with shields up, just to add a level of caution. But I want answers before we even think of getting much closer.

For the moment my adventures in the City by the Bay

*will have to wait. I felt I was close to solving the case
of "Murder at the Stage Door" and finding out who
killed the actress Marci Andrews. But that world can be
put on hold until we discover what faces us. The real
world demands to come first.*

Section Four: Reality Ain't What It's Cracked Up to Be

The narrow, wooden stairs leading up to Cyrus Redblock's second story office creaked under Mr. Data's
weight, no matter how silently he tried to move. He
kept stopping with each step, clearly bothered by the
alarm sounds.

"Go on," Dix said. "If someone is up there, they
know we're here. A few loose boards will make no difference."

Mr. Data nodded.

Dix doubted from what he had seen in the warehouse that they would find anyone alive upstairs. And
he doubted if they would just find the Adjuster sitting
on Redblock's desk, or in a drawer. But they had to
look.

The smell of blood got stronger as they neared the
top, pushing at them, warning them to go back. Bev
covered her mouth and nose with a white-gloved hand.

Mr. Data reached the landing.

Dix nodded to him.

With his big revolver drawn, Mr. Data twisted around
the corner and stepped out of sight into the dark office.

Bev took a deep breath and held it. Dix kept his gun leveled on the landing above them as the seconds seemed to stretch into an eternity.

"Clear, boss," Mr. Data said.

A light came on in the office, filling the top of the staircase with a yellow glow.

Dix had expected the worst inside the office, and that was what greeted him. Three were dead, with dried blood splattered everywhere, as if some kid had gone crazy with dark brown paint. The walls were smashed and pockmarked with bullet holes, the desk overturned, the couch ripped apart. Two streams of blood had formed a small pool on the hardwood floor.

"None of them are Cyrus Redblock," Mr. Data said.

"Well, it seems my information was correct," Dix said. "Redblock has been snatched, and his gang is wiped out."

"Why?" Bev said, moving up to stand beside Dix as they studied the carnage.

"Power and control," Dix said. "It has become a war. Whoever did this is out to take over the city, and until that is accomplished, there's going to be a lot of killing."

"The Heart?" Bev asked.

"More den likely," Mr. Data said, "snatched by da same person who did da killin' here."

Mr. Data hitched up his pants and tucked his gun back in its holster under his arm.

Dix just shook his head. Mr. Data might be right. And he might not be. They needed a lot more information before jumping to that conclusion.

"So what do we do next?" Bev asked.

"We do a quick search of the office," Dix said. "Just to make sure the Heart wasn't brought here before this happened."

Two minutes later they were convinced it wasn't in the office anywhere. Data had even opened the safe hidden behind the picture of a sunset.

"Let's get out of here," Dix said. He wasn't going to allow himself to be disappointed. That would blur his thinking too much. For the next few hours he needed to be thinking as clearly as any private detective had ever thought.

At that moment something bounced on the hardwood floor near the wall.

Mr. Data spun around, his gun back in his hand faster than any quick-draw fighter in the old West.

A moment later something else dropped to the floor and bounced.

Dix stared at it, not believing what he was seeing. A spent bullet had just popped out of the wall.

Twenty-four hours before
the Heart of the Adjuster is grabbed

Captain's Log.
The Enterprise *is drifting in space. We have managed to maintain most internal systems and environmental controls, but warp core went unstable and Engineer La Forge managed to get it shut down before it had to be jettisoned. The magnetic constraints of the impulse*

drive have also become unstable, leaving us only with docking thrusters.

Many other of the ship's systems are having problems, but so far we have kept the essential ones going. It would seem, although none of my people have yet to confirm my suspicion, that the Blackness, as the area of space is being called, has a wider reach than we had expected and has caused, in some fashion, both the destabilization of the warp core and the magnetic failure of the impulse drives.

We have less than forty-eight hours until our current speed, slowed by steering thrusters, causes us to enter into the Blackness. At this point we have no idea what would happen. But it would seem imperative that we not enter that area of space without a great deal more information.

Section Five: Ghosts with Guns

Dixon Hill could not believe what he was seeing. And for a man who trusted his ability to see details where others would miss them, that rocked him.

But what was happening should not be happening. Not in this world.

Not in any world.

Bullets, fired into the wall during the snatch of Cyrus Redblock and the wiping out of his gang, were popping back out of the wall, and the holes sealing over, as if the shot had never happened.

So many of the bullets were coming out of the walls, the desks, and the bodies, and bouncing on the wood floor, that it sounded like he was inside a pan of popcorn popping.

"Let's get out of here," Dix said.

With a quick twist he turned the startled Bev around and headed her toward the office door and the staircase beyond.

They were halfway down the stairs when the shout came from below. "Dix!"

It was Mr. Carter.

"Everyone out!" Dix shouted to his people as he and Bev reached the ground floor, followed by Mr. Data.

The body closest to them was moving, the blood running along the cold, hard concrete and back into the man. It was like watching a movie in reverse.

Redblock's men were coming back to life.

"Mr. Stanley, Mr. Carter, get out!" Dix shouted as he and Bev and Mr. Data ran across the large warehouse toward the open door.

Carter did as he was told, followed a moment later by Stanley.

"Not so fast!" a voice said from behind them.

"Freeze!" another voice shouted.

They were thirty paces from the door across the open concrete.

Thirty paces of cold, hard death.

Dix yanked Bev to a stop and turned to face the man who had shouted.

Mr. Data stopped beside him.

Five of Redblock's men were on their feet, with no signs of the bullet holes that had riddled them a few moments before. All had guns leveled on them.

"Reach for the heavens," one of the goons ordered, waving his gun at the ceiling.

Another of the walking dead climbed to his feet and picked up his gun and joined his friends.

"What do we do now?" Bev whispered to Dix.

Mr. Data gave her an answer. "As Henry Gamadge said, 'Always act as if there was going to be a murder.' "

"What?" Bev asked.

Mr. Data shrugged. "These men were killed. They cannot be happy with the situation."

Dix could not have agreed more. This was not a situation normally faced by a streetwise detective.

"Just great," Bev said as yet another dead goon came back to life and joined the party.

"So," Dixon Hill said, putting his hands in the air, "we do as they say. Unlike them, if we die, we stay dead. Remember?"

The Luscious Bev had nothing else to say.

And Mr. Data had no more quotes.

She and Mr. Data raised their hands in the air and the three of them stood there like a picket fence, facing the walking dead.

Outside the open door, so close and yet so far away, it started to rain again.

Clues from Dixon Hill's notebook in "The Case of the Missing Heart"

- Cyrus Redblock has been snatched by an unknown party.
- Benny the Banger wants to rule the city.
- Reality has changed and death is only temporary to those who live in the city.

Chapter Two

Mobsters, Gangsters, and Thugs, Oh My!

Section One: Dealing with the Devil's Assistant

THE RAIN POUNDED on the metal roof of Cyrus Red-block's warehouse like a hundred drummers, making it almost impossible to hear any distinctive beat. It was a constant thunder, gaining in intensity, then fading back, only to come on strong again.

Dixon Hill ignored the noise and worked at the binds that dug into his wrists. The rope was coarse, rough, and pulled tight, locking his arms behind his back. The goon that tied them had also wrapped the rope once around his chest and around the back of the wooden chair. Dix could stand with the chair, but at the moment that would serve no purpose.

Two other walking dead had given the same treatment to the Luscious Bev and Mr. Data, leaving them all in the main area of the warehouse against the wall facing the large door.

Dix knew that Mr. Data could break free at a moment's notice, but the members of Cyrus Redblock's gang standing guard prevented that. Both their guns stared at him like dark, round cat's eyes, never blinking or turning away.

Dix also worried that Mr. Riker and the others would stage an attack on the warehouse to rescue them. Too many good people might get hurt trying that. With luck, Riker and the rest would hold off and give him time to solve this.

So they sat and waited, the rain pounding on the roof as Dix carefully, without being seen, worked to free his ties.

The man who must have been Cyrus Redblock's second in command appeared from down the stairs that led to Redblock's office. He was followed by four others, all with guns drawn, as if someone might try to ambush them in the narrow staircase. After being killed once so far today, these guys were taking no chances.

The thug in charge wore a dapper pinstriped suit and a brown fedora. His jaw was square and his nose looked like it needed punching. He held his hands behind him, as if starting a lecture to a room full of students. There were no signs in the suit of the bullet holes from earlier. Dix figured the guy was lucky at that. The suit must have set him back a pretty penny.

The pounding of the rain faded to a constant background noise as the man approached his prisoners.

"My name is Danny Shoe," the guy said, stopping directly in front of Dix. His eyes were a deep blue and very intense. "So what'd ya do with da boss?"

"We did nothing with him," Dix said. "And you know that. Were we the ones who attacked you?"

"Might have been your men," Shoe said, brushing aside Dix's answer like he was swatting at a fly.

The other goons nodded like puppets all having the same string pulled from above.

"Me and my men came here to offer to join forces with your boss," Dix said, playing the hand that looked like it had the best chance of success. "Seems we was a little late."

He didn't add the detail about all of them being dead just a short time before. No point in rubbing salt in old wounds, even if they were healed.

"And why would da boss want ta join you?" Shoe asked. "He didn't much like bein' partners."

"To stop what you couldn't stop," Dix said, smiling at the blue-eyed guy standing in front of him. "Your boss getting snatched. Like I said, we was too late."

"You knew it was gonna happen?"

Dix stared at the man, giving him his best how-stupid-are-you look. "Of course. The entire city knew. Where were you? Nappin'?"

Dix glanced at Mr. Data and the Luscious Bev and winked.

"More than likely they was out havin' lunch when the word got passed," Mr. Data said.

"My mother even knew about it," Bev said.

Dix just shrugged at Shoe and kept staring at him.

Now the guys with the guns seemed confused. Two of them actually turned and looked at their leader, clearly starting to think it was his fault Redblock had been snatched.

Shoe snorted, again waving away Dix's word with the back of his hand. "So who put the snatch on the boss?"

"I don't know," Dix said. "Don't you? You was here, wasn't ya?"

"Didn't see much of anything," the guy said. "Happened fast."

"Like an inside job?" Dix asked, smiling at the guy.

Now the men standing around with the guns looked even more uncomfortable. One of them said, "Don't be pointin' no finger at us. We took lead for the boss."

"Yeah," the others said like a boys' chorus hitting the perfect note all at the same time. A couple of them even absently touched places they had been shot.

"Didn't say it was any of you," Dix said, smiling at the guy with the blue eyes. "But which one of ya isn't here?"

Shoe kept looking at Dix while all the goons looked at each other like they had never seen the other guy before, their guns waving back and forth like dead flashlights, searching for the person who wasn't there.

Finally one of them said, "Lenny."

The others murmured and nodded, letting Dix know he had hit on the right idea. Now if he could just turn it into a way out of here.

"Lenny," one man said again. "He was guardin' the back door."

"Where the attack came from?" Dix asked.

Everyone in the place knew it was from the back. The guy named Lenny was now doomed, no matter if he had helped or not. Dix didn't much care.

Cyrus Redblock's second in command nodded, then stared at Dix. "So just because ya know dis, what makes ya think we can trust ya? You coulda been the one settin' it up. Workin' with Lenny."

"Because I'm here and your boss isn't," Dix said.

For a moment the only sound in the big space was the last of the rain beating on the roof as the storm passed.

Then from the back a door slammed, echoing like a shot, and half the men turned, guns ready to fire. This was one jumpy bunch of thugs. Of course, they had the right to be jumpy, considering everything.

A guy came in, walking fast. He was short, with black hair and a long nose. His suit was wet and his hair plastered on his head. He came straight up to the guy in charge. "Word on the street is that Joe Morgan did the snatch."

"The Undertaker?" Shoe asked, turning and ignoring Dix for the moment.

"Yeah," the wet messenger said. "I heard it from a good source, who heard it from a good source, that the boss is stashed alive in a casket in Morgan's headquarters."

"So we go in and get him out," Shoe said.

The other thugs shouted their agreement.

"I wouldn't move so fast," Dix said. "You could get your boss killed permanently. And he wouldn't much like that, any more than he liked the fact that you let him be snatched in the first place."

Shoe turned and stared at Dix. "We was caught by surprise. We'll be da ones doing da surprising dis time."

"My point exactly," Dix said. "Let me and my gang work with you."

"And what's in it for you?" Shoe asked.

Dix decided to level with the guy as much as he needed leveling with. "I'm lookin' for a gizmo people call the Heart of the Adjuster. It's about the size of a small ball, shines like it's made out of gold, but it's not. I help you get your boss back, I get his and your help finding my gizmo."

Shoe stared at him, as if he were a man who couldn't read faced with a page of fine print. Finally he nodded. "Deal. Cut 'em loose."

Dix said nothing until the ropes were cut from all three of them, then he stood and faced Shoe.

"You double-cross me," Shoe said, his blue eyes slitted, "you'll be swimmin' with da fishes."

"No double-cross," Dix said, staring right back. "If your boss is being held by this Joe 'the Undertaker' Morgan, we'll get him back."

"A piece of cake," Mr. Data said, doing his tough-guy stance. "Easy as pie. Slicker than a—"

"Whatever," Shoe said, waving away what Mr. Data

was saying. "Get your people and meet us a block south of da Undertaker's headquarters. Be ready ta fight."

With that he turned and strode toward the cars, his men scattering to follow.

It took Dixon Hill, Mr. Data, and the Luscious Bev only a moment to beat a hasty retreat out into the light rain and the dark night of the street.

Twenty hours before
the Heart of the Adjuster is taken

Captain's Log.
The Enterprise *is still drifting in space toward an area we have called the* Blackness. *We have continued to maintain most internal systems and environmental controls, although with each passing hour it seems to take more and more effort. Engineer La Forge offers little hope of getting either the warp core or the impulse drives back on-line until we discover what exactly is causing the problem.*

On that front, Mr. Data has an amazing theory. He believes—and I tend to agree considering the information we have at the moment—that the Blackness *is framed by not just one quantum singularity, but by four, all staying equidistant from the other. Our instruments can see only one from our present location.*

Such a formation, up to this point unheard of in the known universe, would have the effect of not allowing any light to escape from an area of space between the black holes, thus the Blackness. *It would also cause untold rifts in the space-time continuum. If Mr. Data's theory is correct, this ship would not survive entering the* Blackness.

I have instructed Mr. Data to continue his research to find proof that this is what we are facing, and I have ordered Engineer La Forge and all of engineering to find a way to slow the ship down. We must not get close to the edge of the Blackness, *let alone enter it.*

Section Two: An Alley of Blood

The perpetual night of this city by the bay had turned cold, the dampness biting at fingers and cheeks like an invisible animal, not hard enough to draw blood, but with enough force to leave the skin red and angry.

Dixon Hill had the collar of his tan raincoat up around his neck and the belt of his coat pulled tight. His hands were in his pockets, but his ears and nose were still exposed to the cold. At that moment what he wanted more than anything else was for this case to be over, the Heart of the Adjuster safely back in his hands, and to be downing a hot toddy.

In front of him the street leading to Joe "the Undertaker" Morgan's headquarters seemed empty. The buildings along the street were made of stone and brick, not more than three stories tall. The windows were black and empty, like the eyes of a dead man. The fog seemed to drift around the tops of the buildings, threatening to drop down at any moment and put a shroud on the entire city block.

Dixon Hill glanced around. A dozen of his people, including Mr. Data and the Luscious Bev, were scattered along one side of the street near the mouth of an alley. All were armed and hiding back in the shadows and doorways, waiting.

A short distance away Danny Shoe and Redblock's men were moving slowly toward the front door of the Undertaker's funeral home headquarters. A big main entrance opened right onto the street beside a large garage door, clearly made to handle a hearse. Shoe figured he and his men could bust through the front and surprise the entire place. And he wanted to lead with his men.

Dix was more than happy to let him lead. The last thing Dix wanted was for his people to get hurt.

After Shoe had his men in position in alcoves and such near the Undertaker's front door, Dix motioned for his people to start forward down the narrow side alley that led to the back of the Undertaker's headquarters. Dix's job was to make sure no one escaped out the back, especially with Redblock or the Heart of the Adjuster. With luck, Dix figured he would have the small golden ball called the Heart in his hands in a very short time.

The alley felt more like a tall, dark hallway, with doors inside brick and stone alcoves along both sides. Garbage cans littered one side of the narrow corridor and metal fire escapes clung to both walls casting barlike shadows over everything. A dark alley cat rummaged in the garbage of one overturned can, making almost no noise as it searched for survival. Dix was about to join it in that alley, on the same search.

Just as Dix was about to step into the narrow corridor, three of Shoe's goons busted open the funeral home's front door and went in firing.

The rest of Redblock's men followed.

The quiet, cold street had suddenly come alive with the loud explosions of gunfire, so much that the sound seemed to combine into a thunderlike quality, shaking the windows and rattling doors. Lights in windows up and down the street flashed on as the noise awoke the neighbors.

"Get into positions," Dix shouted to his people as they scattered along the length of the alley and into doorways across from the back entrance of the big funeral home.

The entire building seemed to shake with the storm of weapons fire raging inside it. Clearly Shoe and Redblock's men had met some resistance in there. But they had expected it.

Suddenly the back door burst open and three men Dix didn't recognize ran out into the open. All three were packing large weapons. They were so close Dix felt he could almost touch them.

"Freeze!" Dix shouted.

"Drop the heaters!" Mr. Data joined in.

The three were clearly not used to being smart. All

three spun and started firing, the explosions impossibly loud in the narrow alley. One bullet sent stone chips flying right over Dix's head.

Dix fired back, taking down the guy on the left in the dark suit with a single shot. The other two went to the pavement just as quickly under the hail of fire from Dix's people.

Slowly, the battle inside calmed until there was no more firing. No more men tried to escape.

Dix's ears were ringing from the noise. The smell of gun powder and death mixed with the rotting stink of the alley.

"Damn," Bev said, moving forward and kneeling over someone who lay sprawled in a doorway just a few feet from Dix. It was Evans. He had been hit. Steam was coming from the blood flowing on the side-walk.

Dix moved over to stand above Bev as she checked out the young Evans' wounds. The kid was twenty-six, and had claimed a love for this old city, which is why he thought he could help get the Heart of the Adjuster back. Dix just hoped now the kid wasn't going to die here.

"How is he?"

Bev glanced up, not noticing the blood on her hands that seemed black in the poor light of the street. "He needs medical help. Quickly."

Dix turned and pointed at the nearest one of his men. "Mr. Whelan, you and Carter help get Evans out of here."

They both jumped to Bev's side as Shoe came to the door of the funeral home, took one glance at the three bodies on the ground, and motioned for Dix to come in.

"Let me know how he does," Dix said to Bev.

She only nodded as Whelan and Carter picked up Evans and headed down the street, with her following. Dix watched for a moment, then before he turned to join Shoe he motioned for the rest of his men to stay in position. "Any trouble, pull back and report to Mr. Riker. One of you search these three for the Heart."

They nodded.

Dix indicated that Mr. Data should come with him and he headed for the back door of the funeral home.

"Good job out here," Shoe said, indicating the three dead goons on the sidewalk, before turning and moving into the black opening of the funeral home.

"Redblock?" Dix asked as he followed Shoe into a dimly lit hallway that smelled of disinfectant and even more blood.

"We're workin' on that," Shoe said.

"Working on that?" Dix asked, not liking the answer.

"Does not sound promising," Mr. Data said from behind him. Dix had to agree. Something had gone wrong here.

The hallway opened up into a back storage area of the funeral home. Two men lay dead there, covered in supplies that had fallen from the shelves. Shoe went on through an open door into the casket display room.

"Search this area and these men for the Heart," Dix said to Data, pointing at the storage.

Dix then followed Shoe. Two of Shoe's men had a skinny man in a black suit pressed down into a coffin. Five or six of Shoe's goons stood guard over four of the Undertaker's men near the front door. Even though the room was full of caskets, there were no bodies in here that Dix could see.

"Let him up," Shoe said. "Get him out of there."

Shoe's two stooges yanked the skinny guy up and out of the casket like so much tissue paper, setting him down on his feet.

The thin man swayed for a moment, then caught his balance and straightened his tie, squaring his shoulders to face Shoe.

"So, Undertaker, where's Redblock?"

The thin man shook his head, smiling at Shoe with a sickening mouthful of rotten teeth. "From what I heard, he was snatched right out from under your nose. But not by me."

Dix, for some reason, instantly hated the guy. More than anything he wanted to punch him, but held back.

Shoe clearly didn't feel like restraining himself. He simply stepped forward and buried his fist into the thin man's stomach. With a whoosh of air, the Undertaker doubled over as if he had suddenly lost something on the ground.

"How can I be sure of dat?" Shoe asked.

Dix knew there was no chance the Undertaker could answer that question with all his air gone.

Shoe's goons hauled the thin man back upright. The man's face was red, his eyes bulging out of his face as he fought to catch his breath.

"I asked ya a question," Shoe said, smiling at the Undertaker.

"Search all you want," the thin man managed to choke out. "He's not here. I didn't snatch him."

At that moment Mr. Data came out of the back room. It was clear to Dix that he had not found anything.

The Undertaker took a deep, shuddering breath and again straightened his tie. "As your boss would tell you if he was here, we worked together. Who do you think handled all the bodies your organization generates?"

"Boss!" one of the goons shouted from the front door. "We got company. It's the cops!"

"It would seem," Mr. Data said, "that the gig is up."

> *Eighteen hours before*
> *the Heart of the Adjuster is pilfered*

Captain's Log.
Mr. Data has confirmed, by managing to alter sensors enough to get some basic readings, that the Blackness *is caused by four quantum singularities, all balanced on the same plane like four corners on a square. Such a formation has been theorized as possible since the early twenty-first century, but never seen before now. If this was not affecting our ship and*

*endangering the lives of my crew, it would be a
fascinating scientific study.*

*Mr. Data mapped for the crew the extent of the
subspace disturbances. It would seem that we stumbled
right into it. And with each passing moment we are
going deeper and deeper. We are able to deal with the
forces near a single quantum event horizon, but the
subspace disturbances that are combining from four
are creating a new problem.*

*At least knowing in general what forces we are
dealing with will help in the search for a way to slow
us down to a stop, and then back us away. It would
seem, from Mr. Data's calculations, that at our current
speed, we have forty-two hours before the intense
gravitational forces in front of us tear the ship apart.*

Section Three: Captured Dead or Alive?

"Come on out with your hands in the air!"

The police shout from the street in front of the Undertaker's building echoed like a nightmare for Dixon
Hill. Around him the smell of the funeral parlor closed
in, as if too many bottles of bad perfume had been
opened at once.

The Undertaker laughed. "It would seem we are all
going to be spending some time together."

"They're not going to take us alive," Shoe said.

All of Redblock's men nodded, as did most of the Undertaker's as well. Dix didn't like the looks of that. The
worst thing he could imagine now would be getting in a

gunfight with police. The second worst would be to end up in jail, with what little time they had left ticking away.

"Sir, you have already died once today," Mr. Data said to Shoe. "Don't you think that would be enough?"

"And rot in some stinking jail cell?" Shoe said, staring at Mr. Data. "I'd rather die a dozen times."

"Fighting the police will take you a step toward that goal," Mr. Data said.

Shoe ignored him. He turned to his men guarding the prisoners. "Let 'em go and give 'em back their heaters."

Then Shoe turned to the Undertaker. "Seems we're working together again. Sorry for da misunderstandin'."

Shoe tossed him a gun, and in one smooth motion the Undertaker caught it, turned it around, and shot Shoe at point-blank range.

Before Shoe's body could hit the floor, the Undertaker said, "You are forgiven."

Silence smothered the room like a heavy blanket on a warm summer's day. No one moved.

The Undertaker glanced around at all the men in the room. "Now you're working for me, and if you want to get out of here alive, follow me."

The Undertaker turned and headed for one side of the room where three caskets sat against a wall, their lids closed. He pulled one casket aside, showing a hidden doorway in the wall behind it.

The Undertaker glanced back at the group of goons. "Well, are you all coming?" Then he ducked inside and vanished in the darkness.

Dix watched as Shoe and Redblock's men stood facing the Undertaker's men, keeping their guns trained on each other. Finally one of Shoe's men shrugged and moved to follow the Undertaker into the secret passage. Everyone else did as well, leaving Dix and Mr. Data standing over Shoe's body, alone in the casket-filled area.

"Well, Boss?" Mr. Data asked.

Dixon Hill looked around, trying to give himself a moment to think this all through. He was convinced the Heart of the Adjuster wasn't here. But if not here, then where? Who had taken it, and who had taken Cyrus Redblock? They were no farther along in solving any of this.

"One more warning!" the voice came from a bullhorn out on the street. "Come on out of there with your hands in the sky!"

Dix knew they could not afford the time stuck in jail answering questions. Finding the Heart and getting it out of this city had to take priority over everything.

Suddenly from outside, a massive gun battle broke out, the sound echoing through the building like rolling thunder. It seemed as if the Undertaker's secret escape route hadn't worked as well as planned.

"It would seem the cops have their hands full," Dix said, smiling at his friend. "And that gives us a chance to make our own escape. Follow me."

Outside the gun battle raged on as Dix took the stairs up to the second floor of the building two at a time, then on up to the third and finally up one more flight and out onto the roof.

The cold night air caught him hard, like a slap to the face. The mist and fog swirled around the dark roof, making the pipes and fans that stuck out of the black tar surface seem like graveyard monuments. The gun battle still raged in the street below, sending wave after wave of explosions echoing over the nearby buildings. Not even the fog seemed to dampen the sound.

Flashing red lights of police cars lit up the mist in both directions down the street, making the street feel more like a main boulevard on a Saturday night than a quiet side street.

Dixon Hill moved over to the waist-level stone wall that looked out over the alley and studied what was below. A metal fire escape clung to the side of the building, ending just out of reach above the alley floor.

"Boss, if we go down, we will be trapped in the alley," Mr. Data said. "The cops have the front blocked."

He pointed down through the swirling mist to where two police were stationed in a doorway near the mouth of the alley, firing back up the street, their guns flashing in the faint light.

"Looks like our people got out in time, though," Dix said. "I'm not thinking of going that way." He pointed across the narrow alley to the next building. "See how the landing of the fire escape one floor down sticks out over the alley toward the landing of the fire escape of the other building? There can't be more than ten feet between the two. We go down there, across, and up onto the roof of the building next door."

"The distance between the two platforms is twelve feet," Mr. Data said, "to be exact, boss."

A stray bullet ricocheted off the building and chipped stone from the roof's edge five feet from Dix. He ignored it. This wasn't the time to start being cautious.

He studied the two metal fire escape landings. Making the jump might be possible, but it would make noise, and even with the gun battle going on in the street below, noise at the wrong time would bring attention, and they would be sitting ducks on that fire escape. They'd be cut down before they could climb to the next roof.

He studied the metal of the fire escape. He didn't much like the idea of jumping in the dark and trying to grab on to cold, wet, metal bars. One slip and the two-story fall to the concrete would be painful, at best.

He turned away from the edge of the building as below the gun battle seemed to gain in intensity, as if the police had brought in more men. The rooftop was lit by the neighboring lights and police lights reflecting off the swirling mist. It made everything stand out in stark shadows that seemed to flicker and wave.

Then Dix saw what he had hoped he would see. Against the side of the area that covered the stairway were long planks, clearly used for scaffolding at some time in the past, from the looks of the paint splattered all over them. With Mr. Data at his side he moved to the material and dug out one board. "This long enough?"

"It is, boss."

Quickly they carried the thick, heavy, wooden plank back over to the edge. It was wet and slick from being outside for so long. Slowly they worked it over the edge until it was hanging down along the side of the building with both of them holding it above the landing.

"I'll hold it while you get down there," Dix said, adjusting his grip on the wood so that when Mr. Data let go, he could keep the heavy wooden plank in place. "Be quiet getting it across to the other fire escape."

"You can count on me, boss," Mr. Data said. "Ready?"

"As ever," Dix said.

For a moment, when Mr. Data let go, Dix thought the heavy wooden board would drag him right over the edge. But he managed to brace himself against the stone and hold on as Mr. Data silently went over the edge and down the ladder to the fire escape landing below.

It seemed like an eternity that he held that wood, his hands slipping, his back straining not to let it fall. One slip and the police would see them and then, as Mr. Data had said, "the gig would be up." In a very real fashion.

Somehow, he held on.

Then, as quickly as the weight of the wood had hit him, it was relieved as Mr. Data took the heavy board.

Dix let go and leaned over to watch as Mr. Data silently levered the board out and over the alley, nestling it into place on the other fire escape to form a bridge between the two buildings.

Then he smiled up at Dix and gave a thumbs-up sign.

Dix motioned for him to go across as he swung over the edge and went down the wet, cold, metal ladder that clung to the stone face of the building.

By the time he reached the platform, Mr. Data was standing on the other building's fire escape, looking as calm and collected as if he'd been out for a Sunday stroll in the park.

Dix jumped up on the board, not letting himself look down. Mr. Data steadied it and Dix made it across in four quick steps, not even giving the hard pavement below a glance.

"Stand the board up on this side against the building," Dix told Mr. Data as he started up the ladder toward the roof. "That way no one will notice that anyone got out this way."

Mr. Data levered the board up and stood it on the landing, leaning it against the stone wall of the building as Dix climbed the ladder. Then Mr. Data quickly joined Dix on the roof.

Up the street the gunfight was still filling the night with the sounds of gunshots. The flashing red lights of the police cars made the fog almost blood red. Dix could see a few police bodies in the street. It was clear that the Undertaker and his gang were not going easily.

With Dix leading, they found the way off the roof and down the staircase inside what looked to be an apartment building. On the first floor they came up behind a crowd of residents, mostly dressed in their night-clothes, standing inside the entrance out of the line of fire, trying to watch.

"Careful, folks," Dix said as he pushed through the crowd. "You don't want any stray shots to hurt anyone."

Without waiting for an answer, or any questions as to where they had come from, Dixon Hill, with Mr. Data right behind him, went out the front door and down into the street behind police lines, running to stay low behind the police cars to make sure the now slowly dying gunfight wouldn't catch them.

Dix was about to turn away from the fight when it stopped, almost as suddenly as it had started.

The silence filled the street, seeming almost as loud as all the gunshots. Tucked to one side of the street, half on the sidewalk, was Detective Bell's Dodge. Bell had given Dix a lift in the car to a bar where Dix had been searching out a suspect in a case he called, "The Doll-Faced Caper." Riding with Bell had been an experience Dix was never going to forget, or repeat. The guy didn't believe in the word slow.

Detective Bell had been Dix's inside connection with the cops a number of times, on a number of cases. It suddenly occurred to Dix that maybe Bell might be able to give them a lead on who took the Heart of the Adjuster. And since they were no longer inside the police lines, but outside them, he and Mr. Data had nothing to fear from the cops. Dix doubted anyone who had been inside was left alive to put the finger on them.

Dix motioned for Mr. Data to follow him, then moved up to where a cop now stood behind a police car, his gun still hot in his hands from all the firing.

"Need to talk to Detective Bell," Dix said. "Important."

The cop glanced around, gave both him and Mr. Data the once-over, then pointed down the sidewalk to the left. "I think he holed up in the second doorway there."

There was no sign of anyone in that doorway, but Dix just nodded his thanks to the cop and moved forward. Down the street he could see a dozen cops moving in around the bodies of what looked like the Undertaker and his men.

When Dix reached the deep alcove where Bell was supposed to be, he at first saw nothing. Then the image came clear. In the shadows at the base of a large wooden door, Detective Bell sat, holding his stomach. Black-looking blood dripped through his fingers.

"Call for help," Dix ordered Mr. Data. Then he knelt beside his friend.

Bell looked up, taking a moment to understand who he was seeing. Then he smiled and coughed. "Should have known you'd be around someplace. I'm amazed you weren't in the middle of the fight."

"Don't talk," Dix said. "Help is on the way."

"Not much help for me," Bell said. Then he coughed again, wincing in the pain.

Dix tried to comfort his friend, but from the look of the blood pooled around the detective, he didn't have long.

Bell glanced up after the coughing fit passed. His

eyes seemed extra bright in the dark alcove. "Dix, make sure my wife and kids are all right, would you?"

"Of course," Dix said, squeezing his friend's shoulder. "You know I will."

"Thanks," Bell said. Then he smiled and the light left his eyes and he slumped sideways.

Behind Dix two cops entered the alcove. Dix stood and stepped back, giving them room to check on their boss.

"Oh, no, not Bell," one cop said.

"Were we too late?" Mr. Data asked Dix as they stepped back out into the dark, wet night.

"This time around," Dix said. "This time around."

A slight wind swirled the fog lower among the buildings, and the cold bit even harder at Dixon Hill's face and hands. Especially his blood-covered hands.

Clues from Dixon Hill's notebook in "The Case of the Missing Heart"

- Lenny might have been the inside man on the Redblock snatch.
- The Undertaker worked for Redblock.
- Detective Bell is dead.

Chapter Three

What's a Castle Doing Here?

Section One: The Long Ride

THE COLD OF THE NIGHT AIR chilled Dixon Hill. His breath was a cloud of white hanging in front of his face. He couldn't remember it ever being this cold in the city by the bay. But considering everything that was happening, unusual weather was the least of his problems.

He and Mr. Data and the other four members of his group watched them load the bodies of Joe "the Undertaker" Morgan and six of his goons who died in the street into a white morgue truck. Two other trucks were doing the same thing with other bodies, one truck for the four dead cops, one for the bodies inside the funeral home, including Danny Shoe. As one cop said, "It's goin' ta be a party at da morgue tonight."

Dix wondered if the cop knew just how true his words might turn out to be.

A crowd of neighbors stood on the sidewalks, wrapped against the cold, watching, like a crowd at a baseball game, waiting for something to happen. Dixon Hill half expected there to be a scoreboard on one side of the street: *Gangsters: 12. Cops: 4.* It looked like the game was over for the moment. The half dozen or so gangsters who had been captured alive had already been hauled off to jail.

From down the street Dix saw the Luscious Bev, Mr. Whelan and two others heading his way. As she got close she nodded and smiled, indicating that Mr. Evans was going to make it. Now the scoreboard would read: *Gangsters: 12. Cops: 4. Good guys: 0.*

Dix felt the weight of that worry lift off his shoulders. The kid had been far too young to die.

"Thank you," he said to Bev.

"You're welcome," Bev said, squeezing his arm through his coat. "He's going to be in bed for a few days, but otherwise fine."

"So what's up next, Boss?" Mr. Data asked.

"We're going to make sure we haven't missed anything," Dix said, staring at the funeral home. "Mr. Whelan, I want you and two others to stay here until the police clear out, then search that building for any sign of the Heart of the Adjuster. There are secret passageways, so check everything, including the caskets."

Whelan nodded. "We'll tear the place apart, boss."

Dix nodded, then turned to Carter. "I want you to

take the others, except for Bev and Mr. Data, with you. Search Redblock's headquarters in the same way. Miss nothing. We all meet back in my office."

"Gotcha," Carter said. He pointed to the men standing behind Bev and they headed off down the street, disappearing into swirling fog a half block down the street.

"Mr. Data, Bev, I want you two with me at the morgue. If my friend Detective Bell does what Redblock's gang did, and comes back to life, we could use his help."

"And if he doesn't?" Bev asked, her big eyes shining in the light from the nearby window, her breath swirling in a small white cloud.

"Then we try to figure out what the police know, and go from there."

"In other words, we're playin' it by ear," Mr. Data said. "Goin' by the seat of our pants. Spittin' in the dark. Wingin'—"

"We get the picture, Mr. Data," Bev said.

"The big picture, Toots," Mr. Data said, taking his tough-guy stance again. "The big picture."

Bev just huffed.

Dix stared at the morgue truck that held Detective Bell's body. It looked as if they were about ready to close the door. He turned to Bev. "I'll meet you two downtown. Get there as quick as you can."

He walked toward the truck, and then, just as a cop was about to close the door, he nodded to the guy and climbed into the back.

"You sure you want to ride in there, Hill?" the cop asked.

"Detective Bell was my friend," Dix said. "I'll take the last ride with him."

The cop nodded and moved to close the big doors.

Four bodies, covered in white sheets, filled the space on wire bunklike racks on the walls on both sides of the truck. Dix didn't really look at them as he moved past the dead and sat down on the bench, his back to the cab of the truck.

Then, with a shallow breath, he tried to ignore the smell of blood and death as the cop closed the door and plunged Dixon Hill into darkness.

> *Seventeen hours before*
> *the Heart of the Adjuster is carried off*

Captain's Log.
Mr. Data estimates the Enterprise *now has only forty-one hours remaining until it is torn apart by the forces from the four quantum singularities that form the* Blackness. *Chief Engineer La Forge believes he can keep most of the ship's systems functioning right up to the last minute, but offers no guarantee to the reliability of the more sensitive operations. Even the doors of all the rooms and corridors are opening and closing at random times. Dr. Crusher reports two slight injuries from this problem alone.*

I have assigned La Forge and Mr. Data—and everyone else who has engineering or quantum mechanics experience—to work on a way to block the effects of the Blackness *so that we can restart the impulse drive. The warp core has been completely shut down for safety, so the impulse engines are now our only hope.*

Section Two: Don't Ask

The ride to the morgue in the blackness was a nightmare made real for Dixon Hill. Bouncing through the rough streets, surrounded by four dead bodies, it was everything he could do to keep his mind on why he was riding along on this journey into the depths of the netherworld. The cop driving the truck seemed to pay no attention to speed limits, or bumps, or taking corners too fast. No doubt he wasn't used to having live passengers.

Dix hung on to the metal bench with both hands and tried to float with the moves, even though he had no idea what was coming next. He could hear the bodies bumping against the walls in the darkness with each turn.

Dead flesh against cold metal.

In the dark, that wasn't a comforting sound.

He stopped himself from imagining the truck crashing, the dead bodies flying all around him in the pitch darkness. Instead he focused on what would happen if what was real changed again. If these bodies came back to life, he needed to be with Detective Bell. He needed Bell's help finding the Heart of the Adjuster, and right now the only chance of getting that was to have his friend come back from the dead, as Redblock's goons had done.

Dix didn't much like his chances. In this world of shifting cold and rain and fog, no rule seemed to be firm, no reality functioned exactly the same from moment to moment. Alive or dead, sometimes the line between the two was thin. It seemed it had always been that way in the city by the bay. But now it had gotten worse.

The only certainty was that if Dixon Hill didn't find the Heart of the Adjuster, and get it out of this city, nothing would survive.

The truck took a hard corner, bounced over what seemed like a curb, and then came to a sliding halt, banging Dixon Hill's head against the wall enough to make his ears ring. Thoughts of taking the driver by the throat crossed his mind.

He was rubbing his head when he heard the moan.

At first he wasn't sure if he was the one doing the moaning, then the back doors of the truck flew open and it was clear he wasn't the only live person now riding in the back of this morgue truck. Bullets that had been in the cop's bodies were scattered around the floor. The blood that had stained a few of the white sheets had vanished.

"We're here," the driver said like a conductor on a train announcing the next station as he opened the second door. Then he froze as he looked up into the truck and saw his passengers.

Dixon Hill could only imagine what he was thinking,

or the nightmares the guy was going to live with. All four of the cops that had been dead were now trying to sit up. Two still had the white sheets covering their faces. That was a sight that would haunt anyone's nightmares for years.

The driver made a choking sound and stepped back, his hand on his gun.

"Nothing to worry about," Dix said to the poor, startled man. "They are as alive as you are."

Dix stood and moved to help Detective Bell out of the wire cot hanging on the wall, pushing the white sheet to one side so his legs wouldn't get tangled in it.

"What happened?" Bell asked. "I remember looking up at you in the building doorway, saying something, then it was all nothingness, blackness, like a sleep without dreams." Bell glanced down at where he had been shot, rubbing his hand over his now perfect suit coat.

"You and the rest in here were dead for a short time," Dix said, helping Bell stand and move toward the door.

"I'm in the morgue truck?" Bell asked, shaking his head as he looked around.

"You are," Dix said. "I figure you were dead for an hour at most."

The cop on the ground, his eyes twice the size they should be, kept backing up, his hand on his gun, as if shooting someone who had just come back from the dead was going to help anything.

"How?" Bell asked, glancing around at the other three cops in the morgue van coming back to life.

"I don't know exactly," Dix said, not lying to his friend. "But for the moment, let's just say death for many people in this town is not a permanent thing. That might change at any moment."

"So don't make a habit of getting killed," Bell said. "Is that what you're saying?"

"Exactly, my friend," Dix said, steadying Bell.

Detective Bell half nodded, clearly not understanding, but making the best of the situation, as he always did. Dix knew there was no way he could make his friend understand. They all had to just go with it, as if sometimes returning from the dead was now the reality.

Actually, it was the new reality in the city by the bay, for everyone but Dixon Hill and his people.

"We have one major and immediate problem," Dix said as he and Bell stepped down onto the concrete in front of the city's morgue.

At that moment a second morgue truck pulled in, banging over the curb as the one Dix had ridden had done.

"What's the problem?" Bell asked, "besides me and the others being alive?"

Dix pointed to the other morgue van. "I'm guessing that the Undertaker and his gang, combined with some of Redblock's men, will be back with us as well."

Suddenly Bell became a full-scale detective again. He stood up straight, took a deep breath, and then glanced at the cop who had driven the van. "Keep the back of that truck locked!" Bell ordered, pointing at the one that had just arrived. "And where are our guns?"

"Storage locker right there," the driver managed to choke out, pointing inside the truck. He looked as if he might throw up at any moment.

Bell turned around to one of the cops who had been killed, who was now standing behind him. "Get inside the station and get us help out here. Quick!"

Then Bell pointed at the other two now revived cops, one who was still lying on the bunk. "Get our weapons out of the locker there. Hurry."

"What's the point?" one of them asked. "We shoot them, they just come back anyhow."

"Better than us being shot," Bell said, rubbing the spot on his chest where he had been hit. "Maybe the next time we don't get a second chance."

That got both men moving.

At that moment the third morgue truck pulled in, followed by a number of police cars, their flashing red lights off.

"Bell!" one of the cops said as he got out of his cruiser. "I thought you were dead."

"I was," Bell said. "No time to explain now, even if I knew what was happening. All the guys you shot in those two morgue trucks are alive as well."

"Not a chance," the cop said. "I kicked a couple of the bodies myself, just to make sure."

About ten cops were now standing, facing Bell and Dix. All of them nodded.

"Well," Detective Bell said, "I'm standing here, so you better figure the Undertaker and the rest will be alive as well."

Dixon Hill was impressed at how fast his friend took charge, even though he didn't really understand what had happened. Like any cop, he had seen his share of unbelievable things, and was just treating this like another. He'd figure it out later over drinks down at the corner bar. Probably a few dozen drinks.

The cold air and the swirling low fog overhead swallowed what little noise filled the streets. The cops just stared at their once-dead friend, not sure what to do, or what to believe.

Then someone banged something inside one of the morgue trucks. Someone who should have been dead.

Every cop had his gun in his hand instantly as they spread out facing the backs of the two morgue trucks holding the Undertaker and his goons.

At that moment a dozen more cops came pouring out of the front door of the police station, their guns drawn. They also took up positions behind the two morgue trucks. Bell ordered that a few of the cruisers should aim their front lights and spotlights at the back of the trucks, to blind whoever might be in there.

Finally, when it looked as if everyone was ready, and the lights were on, he motioned for one cop to open one door.

As the door swung open, it didn't surprise Dix to see the Undertaker standing there, shielding his eyes from the sudden bright light.

"Hands in the air!" Bell shouted. "Or we'll blow your heads off and make sure they don't get reattached."

Every man in the van shot his hands into the air, and ten minutes later the gangsters were all sitting in cells.

Even the Undertaker had to admit, being in jail was better than lying on a slab at the morgue.

Fourteen hours before
the Heart of the Adjuster is swiped

Captain's Log.
Engineer La Forge informs me that he thinks he has come up with a way to block enough of the subspace waves coming from the Blackness *to safely restart the impulse drives for a short time. But there are problems involved. The device uses Auriferite, a goldlike substance we keep in small supply in our stores to help in the growth of different plants and the preservation of some alien plant types. For some reason, this substance, when broken down in the correct fashion, forms a subspace shield against the type of disturbance coming from the* Blackness.

La Forge is convinced we have enough Auriferite to do the job, but only barely. His worry is that he may destroy our only supply if his device does not work correctly. He wants to be sure it will function exactly as he wants it to function. I have told him I agree. He will continue testing, while Mr. Data and the rest of the engineering staff look for other methods to extract us, including setting up a promising adjustment to the deflector screens.

Section Three: Wet, Spent, and Little to Show

Grilling Joe "the Undertaker" Morgan was a hot and tiring job. Dixon Hill had long since taken his outer jacket and suitcoat off and loosened his tie. Sweat stained his shirt and he was constantly wiping beads of moisture off his forehead. And he wasn't even the one sitting under the hot light.

The Undertaker was a man far too skinny for his black suit. The guy's thinning hair was plastered to his head like strands of wet string and his mouth hung open like a dog's, clearly dry and needing water. He smelled of rotting teeth and embalming fluid, a smell that got worse the hotter he got.

For almost an hour Detective Bell and Dixon Hill had fired questions one after another, like a machine gun with unlimited ammunition. Hill was starting to think that the Undertaker knew nothing more than he claimed. He said he didn't know who had put the snatch on Cyrus Redblock and killed his men. He hadn't known about it until an hour after it happened.

And worse news to Hill, the Undertaker claimed he had never heard of a gizmo called the Adjuster, or a small gold ball called the Heart. And just like with who snatched Redblock, the Undertaker claimed he had no idea who might have the Heart.

Finally, after Bell had repeated the same question for

the tenth time, and the heat of the overhead light had drained the last sweat from the thin Undertaker's body, he seemed to break.

"Okay, look," the Undertaker managed to say, his voice croaking from lack of water, "I give you a name who might know and you leave me alone?"

"Maybe," Bell said, his face inches from the Undertaker's nose.

"Ghost Johnson," the Undertaker said. His head dropped forward, as if just saying the name had cost him his last energy.

Bell stepped back and glanced over at Dixon Hill.

Dix had never heard of a Ghost Johnson, but it was clear that Bell had. And he didn't like the sound of the name.

"You sure about Ghost Johnson?" Bell asked the Undertaker.

The guy only nodded his head.

The questioning went on for another half hour, with Bell and Hill getting less and less from the thin man. Finally, when it became clear they were getting nowhere, Detective Bell wiped the sweat off his face with his sleeve and banged on the door for the cop outside to come in. "Take him to his cell. Hose him down first."

A big man with a shiny badge entered and walked up to the prisoner, towering over him like a parent over a small child.

"Hey, you can't hold me," the Undertaker complained as the cop roughly hauled him out of the chair under the bright light. "I ain't done nothin'."

"Killin' cops is a lot more than nothin'," Bell said, the disgust in his voice clear and very hard.

"I don't see no bodies," the Undertaker said, suddenly having more energy than he had had for the past hour. "Seems you is walkin' around just fine."

Bell laughed. "No thanks to you and your men. You're goin' away so we have one less piece of trash cloggin' the gutter." Bell nodded to the big cop. "Get him outa here."

The Undertaker tried to twist out of the grasp of the cop, but his thin frame was easy to control for the big man. The cop slammed the Undertaker into the wall beside the door, then said, "Oh, excuse me."

Bell and the big cop both laughed as the big man yanked the thin Undertaker out of the room.

Bell flipped off the hot interrogation light and turned on the room's regular light. Hill slipped on his suit coat and straightened his tie as the temperature of the small room dropped, the heat flowing out the door and into the cooler front area of the station house.

Hill was glad they had at least gotten another lead. From what the Undertaker had said, if he was to be believed, it was doubtful Hill's people had found anything in their searches of Redblock's headquarters and the Undertaker's building. And right now, with time ticking away, any lead was better than nothing.

"So where do I find this Ghost Johnson?" Hill asked.

"You don't," Bell said, slipping on his suit jacket and then tossing Hill his raincoat.

"I got no choice, my friend," Hill said, standing in Bell's way.

"This Heart gizmo is that important, is it?" Bell asked, staring into Hill's eyes.

"More than I could ever explain," Hill said.

"Not much of an answer for a friend," Bell said.

"About all I can say," Hill said. "Except that I can tell you that it concerns what helped bring you back to life."

Bell looked stunned. "You mean whoever controls this gizmo has the power of who lives and who dies?"

"In a manner of speaking," Dix said, "yes." He didn't want to try to explain to his friend that the life of the entire city depended on finding the Heart of the Adjuster. No point in getting into all that and just confusing the issue.

Bell pushed past Hill and stepped into the front area of the police station. It felt like walking into a cooler on a hot summer day. Hill saw that Mr. Data and Mr. Carter were both there, waiting.

Hill put on his raincoat and adjusted the collar as he moved over to Mr. Data. "Any luck?"

"The search of the Undertaker's headquarters was interrupted by the police," Mr. Data said. "The Heart of the Adjuster was not found in Redblock's headquarters."

Bell glanced at Hill. "Doin' a lot of takin' the law into your own hands, Dix."

"Figured you were busy, so I'd have my people do the legwork while we grilled the Undertaker."

Bell laughed. "Yeah, right."

"So where do we find this Ghost Johnson?" Hill asked.

"Ghost Johnson?" Mr. Data asked, looking first at Hill, then at Detective Bell.

"He's the only name the Undertaker gave us," Hill said.

"I don't think taking on Ghost Johnson would be a bright idea," Bell said.

"As Dr. Trevis Tarrant observed," Mr. Data said, " 'When there is only one possibility, it can't be wrong.' "

Hill glanced at Mr. Data. Clearly he had read every mystery he could find. And could now quote the detectives from those books with ease.

Detective Bell just laughed. "I suppose you might be right. But understand that with Redblock out of the way, this city is at war. There are goin' to be dozens of people tryin' to take over Redblock's spot as crime boss. Benny the Banger, Harvey Upstairs Benton, Slippery Stan Hand. And the worst of the bunch by far is Ghost Johnson."

"And the most likely to have put the snatch on Redblock?" Dix asked.

Bell shrugged. "Redblock and Ghost hated each other, but they stayed in their own areas and respected each other's turf. But somethin' might have changed to make him put the move on Redblock?"

"Something like the Heart of the Adjuster?" Hill asked, staring at Detective Bell.

Bell nodded slowly. "All right, we go, but we do this my way."

"And how is that?" Dix asked. They couldn't afford the time to go through official channels for anything.

"You just let me worry about that," Bell said. "But we go in just the two of us."

Dix patted his old friend Detective Bell on the back. "I'm glad you're still alive and with us, my friend."

Bell laughed. "No more than I am."

Twelve hours before
the Heart of the Adjuster is pinched

Captain's Log.
I have ordered all nonessential areas of the ship to be shut down due to the recent emergency. For twelve minutes and eight seconds, all ship's environmental controls were off-line. No crew were injured or in any immediate danger, but the failure clearly illustrates the gravity of our situation.

Chief Engineer La Forge has asked permission to use a fraction of the available Auriferite to create a blocking barrier around the main environmental controls, to keep them working. He does not believe that such use would jeopardize the possibility of starting the impulse drives.

I agreed and he has just informed me the Auriferite blocking device is in position and blocking most of the effects of the Blackness. *But not all of them. That is not a good sign in my opinion, but La Forge does not seem concerned.*

When we return to base, I will ask La Forge to submit detailed information as to his discovery of the subspace properties of Auriferite. The long-term implications of such a simple discovery may have a lasting impact on science and the defense capabilities of the Federation.

However, first things first. We must escape this trap we have stumbled into.

Mr. Data, on a second area of research, is about to test a device he has called the Adjuster, which compensates for the subspace disturbances, which he theorizes will allow the impulse drives to function at a low enough level to stop us and back us away from the Blackness. *His test is scheduled in thirty minutes.*

Section Four: There's a Light . . .

By the time Dixon Hill, Detective Bell, and the others had reached the side street that led out to Ghost Johnson's headquarters, the fog had lifted and the cold had eased. Now the sky was clear and the stars were out, shining like dandruff on a black suit. Only a few fast-moving clouds slid by overhead, lit by the lights from the city.

Dixon Hill could never have imagined things changing so fast. There was an old saying about the weather in the city by the bay. If you didn't like it, wait five minutes and it would change.

Dix hated old sayings like that, and he had heard that same saying about every part of the world. But sometimes those old sayings applied, and tonight, in this city, was one of those times. Dix still hated the saying, accurate or not.

On top of that, this night seemed to be lasting far longer than normal. It was as if daylight didn't exist in this town. Or even time, for that matter. With the way reality was being bent, that was not only possible, but likely. It made Dix feel like he had stumbled into a carnival fun house, where the mirrors distorted your location, the wind whipped at clothing, and the path to the exit was far from clear.

Until Dixon Hill found the Heart of the Adjuster, it seemed he was stuck in a fun house night of changing weather, shifting reality, and perpetual darkness.

The side street that lead to Ghost Johnson's headquarters started out looking a great deal like the street the Undertaker's headquarters had been on. Three-story stone buildings lined both sides, and the windows were dark, making them look empty and dead. The sidewalks framed a narrow street that moved up a slight hill. But when they crossed over the crest of that hill, it became clear the road led out of the city, through some thick trees.

Mr. Data was driving the Dodge, a skill he had mastered during one of Dix's earlier cases. Dix was in the passenger seat, with Detective Bell and the Luscious Bev in the back. Mr. Data flawlessly sped the car down the road as it suddenly turned from pavement to dirt.

"Don't you think you should slow down some?" Bev

asked, leaning forward and grasping onto the back of the seat as the car bounced through a pothole. Mr. Data corrected a slide to the right, going even faster.

Dix had been thinking the very same thing.

Mr. Data laughed in his hard-guy voice. "Toots, as Inspector French once said, 'If we were all as wise as we should be, we would have no stories to tell.' "

"That may be true, Mr. Data," Dix said, grasping the dashboard as Mr. Data slid the Dodge through another corner and then corrected. "But lives depend on us, and we need to reach our destination in one piece."

Mr. Data nodded and slowed the car, just as they broke out of the trees and into the open.

Dix was stunned at what faced them. The road wound through an open area down to what looked like a cliff face over the water. Then the road went along the steep drop-off to what could only be described as a castle sitting on a rocky outcropping. It looked dark and ancient, with only one light in a single window on the second floor.

"A castle?" Mr. Data asked.

"Looks that way," Dix said. He had no idea there were such structures in the area of this city. It looked like it belonged on a coast in Europe.

"That's Ghost's headquarters?" Dix asked.

"That's it," Detective Bell said, leaning forward between Mr. Data and Dix. "Creepy old place, ain't it?"

"Gothic," the Luscious Bev said softly. The word sent chills down Dix's spine.

Dix motioned for Mr. Data to stop the car and he

did, just at the point where the road turned and moved along the cliff face. Even under the dark night sky, Dix could see the waves crashing on the rocks far below his window, the sound almost louder than the car engine. And the smell of the ocean was overpowering, making the air thick and rich, heavy with the dampness.

"So how do we get in there?" Dix asked, glancing around at his friend. It didn't seem possible, without a full-out assault, and Dix didn't want to risk any of his people with that unless he knew for certain the Heart of the Adjuster was inside.

"Easy," Bell said. "Follow me. Mr. Data, you and this wonderful woman stay in the car."

Detective Bell then opened the back door of the car, letting in the sound of the ocean like turning up a hi-fi.

Mr. Data glanced at Dix, who nodded. "Go for help if we're not out in an hour."

"Gotcha, boss," Mr. Data said, turning off the car, which had the effect of making the ocean pounding on the rocks sound even louder.

"Be careful in there," Bev said, putting a hand on his shoulder.

Dix patted her hand. "Don't worry."

"Yeah, right," Bev said. "What's there to worry about?"

Dix laughed and got out, standing beside the car not more than five feet from a long drop to very sharp rocks.

Both Mr. Data and Bev got out of the car as well and moved to stand in front of it where Bell waited. Dix joined them, glad to be getting more distance between himself and that cliff. He normally was not bothered by heights, but tonight, on this bluff, in this darkness, it felt dangerous.

The car's headlights shaped them, brightly lighting one side while leaving the other half of their bodies in blackness. It was a strange look. But Dix liked how it made Bev look alluring and mysterious.

"Coming, old man?" Detective Bell asked Dix. Then, like he was out for a Sunday walk in the park, Bell started out, heading up the road toward Ghost Johnson's castle on the rocks as if he didn't have a care in the world. Or a brain in his head.

"If there are problems," Dix said to Mr. Data, "have everyone report to Mr. Riker."

"Right-o, boss," Mr. Data said. "Keep your hand on your piece and your legs together."

Dix looked at his friend. He had no idea what he meant.

Mr. Data only shrugged.

"You comin'?" Bell asked, stopping just outside the light from the car.

Dix nodded and without another word to his companions, moved up the rough dirt and rock road.

"Just act natural and follow my lead," Bell said as they moved along, watching their footing.

Behind them their car seemed to grow smaller, as if climbing the hill was taking them a farther distance away than it should have. And in front of them the castle loomed into the sky, growing bigger with each step, a threatening stone structure with one light showing no welcome at all.

A wind whipped at them, stronger than it should have been, considering that a hundred paces down the road there had been no wind. A cat dashed across the road, startling Dix before it vanished into the brush on the right.

They kept moving, step after step taking them closer and closer to the castle that loomed large over them.

Suddenly a scream cut the night air, overpowering the sounds of the ocean like a hot knife through soft butter.

"What?" Detective Bell said, his gun instantly in his hand.

Dix also had his gun out, but there didn't seem to be anything happening, and there was no way of telling on this rocky, wind-whipped bluff where the scream had come from.

Dix glanced back down the road. Bev and Mr. Data were both still beside the car. They were acting as if they hadn't heard anything.

The woman's scream cut through the night air again, this time louder and even closer.

Then, as if coming out of nowhere, she was there, running at them.

He dark hair flowed back from her head; her thin white nightgown barely covered her shapely body. She was looking behind her at the castle as she ran, not seeing them.

Then she looked ahead, right at them, and the terror on her face and in her eyes was clear. Dixon Hill had never seen anyone so afraid.

"Hang on there!" Detective Bell shouted to her.

The woman seemed not to hear him.

Or even see them.

She just kept running, right at the cliff face to the right of them, glancing over her shoulder, then back, never slowing, as if something was chasing her in a nightmare.

Around them the night air become arctic, the wind now ice-cold and biting into any exposed skin. Dix felt his skin tingle and his hair stand on the back of his neck. Fear ripped at him, as if something wanted him to turn and run.

He held his ground.

Bell stepped toward the woman as if to grab her, stop her flight.

She stepped sideways, dodging his grasp, and went right past him.

Dix jumped to grab her, but she eluded him as well.

A half dozen steps later, with a bloodcurdling scream of terror, the woman in the nightgown flung herself over the edge of the cliff.

Her scream seemed to echo as she dropped, then was suddenly cut off.

And for a moment, not even the ocean made a sound.

Clues from Dixon Hill's notebook in
"The Case of the Missing Heart"

- The Heart is not in Redblock's headquarters, and most likely not in the Undertaker's place either.
- Never ride with dead bodies in a morgue truck.
- Ghost Johnson, Benny the Banger, Harvey Upstairs Benton, and Slippery Stan Hand are the main suspects on the Redblock snatch.
- A woman killed herself in front of Ghost Johnson's headquarters.

Chapter Four

Gothic Suspense Means Never Having to Say You're Sorry

Section One: Who Was That Woman?

DIXON HILL STOOD BESIDE Detective Bell as the cold wind whipped at them, snapping their pant legs, yanking their coats away from their bodies. Below, the ocean pounded into the rocks of the cliff, hammering away so hard that the ground shook. There was no sign of the woman's body. Dix had no doubt she had died from the fall. And even if she had survived, the cold water would soon take her, or pound her to death on the rocks. Not a pretty way to die. If there was such a thing.

"We better get some help out here looking for her body," Bell said, his words snapped away by the wind. "If she's going to come back to life, like I did, she's going to want to be out of that water when it happens."

The thought sent shivers down Dix's spine. No one deserved that fate, dying and then coming back time after time, only to die an ugly death again and again. The possibility of that happening to her hadn't crossed his mind. He had been more concerned about finding out who she was, what she had been running from, and if it had anything to do with the Heart of the Adjuster that he needed to find.

"Maybe Ghost Johnson's would have a phone," Dix said, glancing up at the castle that loomed over them.

Bell nodded. "And maybe he might know who she was."

"And what she was running from," Dix said.

"Yeah, that too," Bell said.

With one more glance over the edge of the high cliff at the black rocks and pounding surf below, Dix turned and headed up the road the last few hundred paces to the front of the castle. Detective Bell was at his side.

They turned off the road and climbed up the steps to a huge, wooden front door that looked like it was large enough to let trucks through. Just as they reached the door and Dix was wondering if they were going to have to knock, a man stepped out of the bushes on the right. He was wearing all black so that he blended into the night like a shadow cast by a faint moon. The gun in his hand was very big and shined like a warning beacon.

As he moved forward a light snapped on, filling the area with just enough light to push back the darkness to the edge of the walkway leading from the road.

"You the one chasing the woman?" Bell asked.

The guy looked at him like he had lost his mind. "You have no business here. Leave now."

"We'd love to," Bell said, "but we have a few problems. A woman just tossed herself off your cliff, so we need to borrow a phone. And we need to talk to Ghost."

"Ghost ain't seein' anyone," the guy said, his voice low and deep and as menacing as the gun he kept pointed at them.

"Tell him Detective Bell is here," Bell said, smiling at the man. "He'll see me."

"You don't hear so well, do ya, fella?" The big guy stepped toward them, his eyes cold and threatening. "Ghost ain't seein' anyone. Especially *cops.*"

The guy almost spit the last word. Dix had no idea what they were going to do now. Somehow they needed to talk to Ghost Johnson and get help on the way to find the woman's body.

With a quick step Detective Bell kicked the gun from the guard's hand, sending it spinning into the air and banging against the wooden door.

Dix snapped his gun out from under his rain coat and had it trained on the big guy before the kicked weapon stopped moving. But it was clear the situation wasn't what Dix thought it was. The guy didn't make a move at Bell, and Bell didn't make a move at him. Instead both of them laughed.

Okay, now Dixon Hill was confused. The laughs from the two men seemed to echo out over the ocean, pulled there by the wind and the very strangeness of it all.

"Pretty good," the big guard said as his laughing slowed and he shook the hand that held the gun, as if it was stinging from the kick, "for a cop who was headed for a morgue slab just a few hours ago."

Dix stared at the guard. A moment before he had been speaking roughly, now his voice was cultured and softer.

"You made it too easy on me," Bell said, then laughed again. He stepped forward and patted the big guard on the back. "How'd you hear about the little death and rebirth problem so fast?"

The guard frowned at Bell. "You know I have connections, Detective. It had me saddened, I must say, until I heard of your *recovery.*"

"I wasn't any too pleased with it myself," Bell said. Then both men laughed again.

All Dixon Hill could do was stand there and stare. It was like he was on some stage, under a spotlight, and he didn't know his part or his lines.

Bell motioned that Dix put his gun away and Dix did as he was told. Then Bell did the introduction. "Dixon Hill, I'd like you to meet Ghost Johnson, the greatest patron of the arts this city has ever seen."

"The Private Eye?" Ghost asked, his eyebrow rising as he stepped forward and shook Dix's hand. "I have heard you are looking for some object that has been lost. Am I correct?"

Dix was shocked. He wasn't sure what he had expected, but this guy clearly didn't follow any of the mob boss patterns in this city.

"Yeah," Dix said. "Lost or taken. It's a small ball, smaller than a woman's fist, painted gold."

Ghost nodded. "That was what I had heard. I'm afraid I haven't seen it. I do so wish I could help you."

Dix nodded, still stunned at the man's cultured voice and attitude. He didn't know if he should just take the man at his word or press forward. Clearly this man could act.

"So what about the dame?" Bell asked. "You know, the one who just did a leap onto the rocks?"

Now Dix could tell it was Ghost's turn to be surprised. "To what woman are you referring? I thought you were joking, as you are wont to do in situations such as this."

Bell looked at Ghost closely, then nodded. "You honestly don't know, do you?"

Ghost shook his head. "I'm afraid I have no idea what you are talking about. When you first mentioned it, I just thought it a ploy to distract me. Part of our little game."

"I wish," Bell said. "As we were walking up the driveway, a woman wearing a very thin nightgown screamed and ran past us. We couldn't stop her before she went over the cliff."

"Clearly something or someone was chasing her," Dix added. "She was terrified. And she appeared to be coming from this direction."

"What exactly was her appearance?" Ghost asked.

"Long dark hair," Bell said. "Dark eyes. Slender, maybe early twenties in age."

"Wearing a white, thin nightgown," Dix added, the image of the woman clear in his mind. It would be a long time before he would forget her. "No shoes or slippers, and completely in terror. Running away from something."

Ghost nodded. "The description does not fit anyone on my staff, but I will gather them at once and inquire."

"And we need to call for some help to search for her body," Bell said.

"I would imagine," Ghost said, "you would want to find her if there is any chance she might return to the land of the living. The phone is inside the door on the left."

Dix followed the two friends toward the front door of the big castle. Clearly the reality of the chance of returning to life was becoming a thought for everyone around him. Amazing how people could quickly adapt to such a large change in perspective. But Dix knew that for his life and his people's lives, there would be no coming back from death. It was just a disadvantage they were going to have to live with until they finished what they had come to do.

Ten hours before
the Heart of the Adjuster is boosted

Captain's Log.
Mr. Data's test of the device he is calling the Adjuster did not go well. From my understanding of our situation, the overlapping subspace disturbance waves

*coming from the four singularities are not forming a
pattern that can be successfully blocked by our
conventional shields. The device Mr. Data is attempting
to make work would adjust our subspace shielding fast
enough to block the waves from each singularity.*

*But as Mr. Data has informed me, the chaos aspects
of the overlapping waves are making such adjustments
almost impossible. He gives little chance for success,
but until we can come up with another method, I have
ordered him to continue his quest along those lines.
Even if he can manage to block the effects of the
Blackness for a few seconds, it would slow our speed
and give us more time.*

*On another front, Engineer La Forge is continuing to
run tests on the capabilities of the Auriferite. We have
thirty-four hours remaining before we enter the
Blackness and are ripped apart by the forces inside
that border. He tells me his tests will be done in the
next few hours. I believe that his discovery of the
properties of Auriferite will be our solution to this
problem situation.*

Section Two: Just Art

The footsteps of Dixon Hill, Detective Bell, and their
host, Ghost Johnson, echoed through the massive main
foyer of the castle. Polished marble floors reflected the
flickering light of a welcoming fireplace against one
wall. A grand staircase, wide enough for five people to
walk side by side, curved up one wall to a second floor

far overhead. Three major arched hallways led away in three directions from the main door, turning in short distances so it was impossible to see how far they went.

The place felt cold and unwelcoming, even with the fire.

Ghost headed for the hallway on the right and Dix and Bell followed. "Impressive place, isn't it?" Bell said, smiling at how Dix was looking around. "Ghost here got it for a steal."

Ghost laughed. "You have that correct, my friend. I purchased it for little more than a song from Barney the Beast, when Bell and his fine forces put Barney up the river for a life sentence."

"It was my pleasure," Bell said. "Glad to help a friend with a real estate purchase."

Dix said nothing as they turned the corner in the hallway, went through two large wooden doors, and into a carpeted library, with leather-bound books stacked on dark wooden shelves two stories into the air. A massive, ornate chandelier and the fire in a large stone fireplace were the main sources of light. Unlike the coldness of the front foyer, this room felt warm and inviting, with three deeply padded couches arranged in front of the fireplace.

Dix glanced at the titles of a few of the books. All great classics, in fine first editions. Dickens, Shakespeare, and Melville were just a few authors Dix recognized as he glanced around. There were also classic mystery and romance as well. Too bad he didn't have a year or two to just curl up in this wonderful room and read. Maybe after this case, he would see if he could at least arrange a visit to this fantastic library.

Ghost moved to a cord hanging near the door and pulled it. Dix half expected to hear a distant bell, but nothing happened.

"The phone is there," Ghost said to Bell, pointing to a small end table to one side of the fireplace. Bell nodded and moved to it, quickly dialing a number.

"This is an amazing collection of books," Dix said to his host.

"Thank you," Ghost said. "I've heard you were a man of learning. Maybe someday I can give you a little tour of the volumes here."

"I would like that very much," Dix said.

A man in a butler's uniform appeared from out of a side door near the fireplace and stopped facing Ghost. The butler was a short man, with gray hair and a large nose. His eyes were the eyes of man who had seen too much. He had the appearance of a butler, but not the feel of one.

"Please have all the staff report to this room at once," Ghost ordered.

The man nodded his head as if in a shallow bow, and turned and left as quickly as he had appeared.

"Should only take a moment," Ghost said, moving across the room.

Bell hung up the phone and turned. "Reinforcements and search crews are on the way. They should be here in fifteen minutes."

"Good," Ghost said, gesturing that Bell and Dix

should be seated on the couches. Dix pulled out his pocket watch and glanced at it. There was still enough time before he needed to check in with Bev and Mr. Data.

"May I offer you gentlemen a snifter of cognac while we wait?" Ghost asked, stopping at an ornately carved wooden bar tucked in between the bookshelves. He picked up a cut glass decanter with a golden fluid and held it out.

"On duty at the moment," Bell said. "But would love to take a rain check."

"As would I," Dix said.

"Suit yourselves," Ghost said. "But I hope you don't mind if I partake?"

"Not at all," Dix said.

Bell laughed. "I sure ain't goin' ta be sayin' no to a man drinkin' in his own home."

Ghost again laughed. "You have a point, Detective."

By the time he had finished pouring himself a small snifter full of the golden liquid, six staff members had filed in through the side door. Each wore the traditional uniform of a servant. Two butlers, one cook, and three maids. All seemed to be much, much older than either Ghost or the woman who had jumped off the cliff.

Dix also noticed that even though Ghost Johnson was supposed to be one of the crime bosses capable of running the city, none of the people who worked for him seemed to carry a gun, and there were no goons, like the ones who worked for Redblock and the Undertaker.

Ghost faced his employees. "Our guests this evening witnessed a young woman throwing herself off the cliff below this building. She seemed to have come from here and to have been very frightened of something. Do any of you have any knowledge of this poor young woman?"

It was clear to Dix that all of them did. All shifted and couldn't meet their employer's gaze. One maid even gulped and went pale.

The reaction was not lost on either Bell or Ghost Johnson. Ghost glanced around at Bell and Dix, a look of puzzlement on his face, then turned again to his employees.

"Well?" Ghost asked, his voice stronger and much more full of authority than it had been a moment before.

The employees glanced at each other and seemed ill at ease, like children caught doing something wrong, but afraid to tell a parent. They were clearly hiding something. Finally, the butler who had answered the cord-pulling summons stepped forward. "I can tell you of the young woman. The others are not needed."

Ghost glanced at his other employees, all standing in a line and looking as if at any moment they might run away screaming. Then Ghost nodded. "Very well. You are all dismissed."

They turned and left quickly, leaving the older butler standing almost at attention in front of the imposing and powerful figure of Ghost Johnson.

Ghost stared at the man for what seemed like far too

long a time. Dix wished he could see the look on Ghost Johnson's face, what was going on between the two, but the butler kept a blank poker face and Ghost had his back turned. Finally Ghost moved over and leaned against the bar, taking a sip of his drink.

Dix could feel the tension in the room thicken. The air seemed to get heavier, the crackling of the fire louder. All three of them stared at the butler.

The butler did not wilt under the stares. In fact, he didn't move, his gaze locked on something across the room in front of him.

"Well, Reston?" Ghost said after the silence grew, pushing at the walls.

The butler nodded and turned slightly to face his boss, ignoring Dix and Bell on the couch. "I am not exactly sure where to start, sir."

"As a great author once advised," Ghost said, "the best place to start is at the beginning and then go until you reach the end."

Reston the butler nodded. "Yes, sir." He took a deep breath. "Just over forty years ago, right at the turn of the century, a young man named Williams lived in this castle. It seems, as rumor has it, that he was very rich, well connected to eastern money, but not very handsome. The society women of the time still considered him the prize catch for their daughters."

Ghost glanced at Bell and Dix, then nodded for Reston to go on with his story.

Dix had a hunch he knew where this story was heading.

Reston continued. "A marriage, of sorts, was arranged between a beautiful young woman and Williams, with a great deal of money changing hands. However, as youth sometimes does, this young woman had a true love she did not want to leave. But at the time, she had no choice, and was married to Williams."

"Let me guess," Bell said, "she and her true love couldn't stay apart."

"You are correct, sir," Reston said. "When the master of the house traveled, as he did a great deal, the two young lovers would meet here. One night Mr. Williams came home unexpectedly and found them together."

Dixon Hill had heard this story before, in a dozen different ways, in hundreds of different books, the only variation being slight details. Also, Reston was not a convincing storyteller, by any means.

Reston, not really taking his gaze from his boss, went on with his poor story. "In anger Williams stabbed the young man and then cut out his heart and offered it to his wife. The sight of her lover's heart, still warm in her husband's hand, sent the woman screaming from the castle in terror, where she met her death by leaping over the cliff and into the ocean below."

Detective Bell snorted and shook his head.

Ghost Johnson said nothing.

The silence in the room was broken only by the soft crackling in the fireplace.

Dixon Hill sat and thought about how it had felt the moment the woman had run past them. The cold had been intense, he would grant that, and there had been a real sense of terror surrounding the woman. Maybe he should believe the story. With all the reality changes going on in this city, having spirits appear and kill themselves right in front of him actually made sense. But there was still something that didn't fit about any of this. And the story was so standard, so cliché, that it felt out of place in a room full of the classics of literature.

"So we saw a ghost," Bell said, laughing. "Is that what you are telling us?"

"Yes, sir," Reston said. "You are not the only ones to have seen her. I have as well, on three different nights."

"Why was I not told of this?" Ghost demanded.

"It didn't seem to be an important topic, sir," Reston said. "She is never seen anywhere but near the cliff, and only at night for a short time."

"Guess I should call off the troops," Bell said, standing and moving toward the phone. "Going to be tough to find the body of a woman who has been dead for forty years. They're going to be laughing at me for a month over this."

Bell's words triggered something in the back of Dix's mind. What a perfect way to cover for a crime. Simply call it a ghost story. But there was one detail about the woman that neither he nor Bell had told Ghost. And it was a critical detail that made her very real. And the terror she had been running from just as real. Or at least as real as anything could be at the moment in this city.

"I wouldn't be so sure of that," Dix said to Bell. "You might have them take a look after all."

"Why?" Bell asked, his hand on the phone. "I'm going to catch enough grief over the first call."

Ghost glanced at his butler, than back at Dixon Hill. "I am wondering the same question. Why?"

Dixon Hill glanced around at the room full of books, at the softly crackling fire, and then back at his cultured mob boss host. "I've come to realize—especially this evening—that things are often not as they appear."

"Meaning what?" Bell asked, his hand still resting on the phone.

Dixon Hill smiled at his friend. "But even though things are not what they seem, sometimes what you see is what you see."

"You don't believe the ghost of the castle bit?" Bell asked.

"Oh, I believe this place has a ghost," Dix said, glancing around. "Why wouldn't it? And I even believe it might be a ghost who tossed herself over the cliff at some point in the past. But what we saw tonight was no ghost. That much I am sure of."

As he was speaking, Dix was watching Ghost Johnson shift slightly.

"And how can you be so sure about that?" Bell asked.

"Yes, Mr. Hill," Ghost asked, picking up his glass and then putting it back down, his hand dropping out of sight behind the bar top as he made the move. "I am curious as well. What is your well-known private investigator's logic seeing that we are not seeing?"

Dix smiled at the frown on his host's face. From the way the man was moving and easing to get into position, Dix knew he was on the right track. "Actually, you would have no way of knowing it wasn't the ghost we saw. Because you weren't there to see her duck around our attempt to stop her."

"By heavens," Bell said, "you're right. She did. No spirit would do that."

At that moment Ghost Johnson reached for what must have been a gun tucked behind the bar, but Dix was faster.

Much faster.

"Don't try it!" Dix shouted. His gun was leveled on Ghost Johnson.

The butler looked at Dix coldly, his eyes nothing more than angry slits.

Ghost Johnson froze, his hand still out of sight behind the top of the wooden bar.

Again, the silence smashed down on the room, broken only by the faint crackling of the fire in the big stone fireplace. The weight of the written words that surrounded them pressed inward, making the air heavy with drama. Again Dix felt as if he were standing on a stage. Only this time he knew his part and his lines perfectly.

And he knew that what they had now was a classic standoff. Everyone in the room knew it.

How long would it last? was the first question.

And how it would turn out the second.

Unlike long-drawn-out scenes in plays, this standoff did not last more than an instant.

Ghost Johnson broke the mood, broke the tension, and broke the standoff by smiling, his white teeth beaming in the firelight.

"You are very astute, Mr. Hill."

"So what was the woman to you?" Dix asked.

Ghost Johnson again smiled. "Only an actress, playing her part."

"Pretty deadly audition," Bell said.

"Art often requires sacrifices," Ghost said. "You, Mr. Hill, as a learned man, must understand that."

With the smile still filling his face, Ghost's hand came up from behind the bar holding his gun as he spun sideways.

Dixon Hill fired, the explosion impossibly loud as everything in the room seemed to move at once.

Ghost also fired, but with Dix's bullet plowing through his chest, the shot was wide and high, ripping through the spine of an old volume of *Wuthering Heights*.

Dix had won that showdown easily.

Reston the butler moved, his hand flashing to his back, appearing an instant later with his gun. Dix turned toward him, but before Reston could bring his gun up into position another shot tore through the room from Bell's gun.

Reston spun and went down, spraying blood on the carpet.

Bell had won the second showdown.

Ghost Johnson slid down the front of the wooden bar and into a sitting position on the floor, the smile on his face still frozen in place. "It would seem that we have switched genres."

Bell moved up and stood beside Dix, staring at Ghost Johnson. "What do you mean by that?"

Ghost coughed, spitting out blood, so Dix answered for him. "A genre is an area of literature, defined by the topic in the story."

Ghost nodded. "Gothic suspense never has a gun-fight in it."

"You were counting on that?" Dix asked.

Ghost laughed slightly, then coughed again. "I never expected you to see her in the first place. This is my private stage, my private narrative, my private art."

"You killed that woman as art?" Bell asked.

"Of course," Ghost said. Then his eyes seemed to lose focus. "All life is a stage, my friend."

"But before you can have art, you must first have audience," Dix said.

"It seems," Bell said, "that this audience just gave you a bad review and put you out of show business."

A gurgling sound filled the library as Ghost Johnson took his last breath and fell over sideways in a very convincing death scene.

*Eight hours before
the Heart of the Adjuster is appropriated*

*Captain's Log.
We have had a possible breakthrough. It started as
Mr. Data attempted to explain to all the senior staff the*

reason the device he is calling the Adjuster is failing. He used an on-screen graphic example of dropping four stones into a smooth pond, at four corners of a square area. He called the waves radiating from the stones dropping representations of the subspace disturbances.

Mr. Data then went on to explain how the waves collide in a certain pattern, creating a new type of wave that carries a different intensity and wave pattern. He explained that the patterns are traceable when only two stones are dropped. And might be possible at three. But when the waves from four different disturbances are constantly colliding and overlapping and bouncing and changing each other, it is impossible to accurately calculate what the force, intensity, and level of disturbance will be at any set point for any set time.

Thus, Mr. Data believes his Adjuster will offer nothing of value in saving the ship.

Chief Engineer La Forge had reported to me earlier that he also was not having much success. It seems that the Auriferite substance blocks some, but not all, of the types of subspace disturbances coming from the four singularities. Not enough, he said, to allow starting of the impulse engines.

As Engineer La Forge sat and listened to Mr. Data explain the difficulties of a computer adjustment to random chaos events he came up with an idea. Stopping Mr. Data, La Forge asked a simple question. "Would it be possible to computer adjust the screens with your device if a large factor of the disturbances were blocked by Auriferite?"

It took Mr. Data a very long three seconds before he responded. "It would be possible. Yes."

I ordered the two to work together and report back in two hours. We now have thirty-two hours remaining. A solution must be found, and found quickly.

Section Three: Back to the Beginning

Dixon Hill stood in the massive entrance foyer beside the Luscious Bev and watched as Mr. Data came down the grand marble staircase beside one of Detective Bell's officers. "I'm afraid, boss," Mr. Data said, shaking his head, "that we have had no success."

At that moment Detective Bell and Mr. Whelan came out of the hallway leading to the kitchen area. "Nothing, Dix," Bell said. "I don't think Ghost had your gold ball gizmo."

"We gave the place a good going-over," Mr. Whelan said.

"As did I," Mr. Data said. "No stone unturned, no rug left smooth, no safe uncracked, no bed left made, no—"

Dixon Hill held up his hand. "We get the idea, Mr. Data. I too don't believe the Heart is here."

"And no sign of Cyrus Redblock either," Mr. Whelan said. "But we did find a few interesting-looking cell areas in the basement behind some secret doors.

"More than likely where they kept the girl," Bell said.

"So what is our next step?" Bev asked.

Dix looked at her. He had no idea what they should do next. Somehow he was sure the abduction of Cyrus Redblock and the taking of the Heart of the Adjuster were related. But finding out who took either seemed to be impossible.

"You know," Detective Bell said, "that Harvey Upstairs Benton might know a thing or two about this."

"Why's that?" Dix asked.

"He specializes in diamonds and gold. Since your gizmo is gold colored, it might be right up his alley."

Dix nodded. It might be a lead. Or it might be like this had been. Another dead end and more lost time in the search for the Heart.

"Detective?" a man said from the open front door. "We found the woman's body."

Bell glanced at Dix. "Give me a call if you need more help." With that he headed out the door and down the front sidewalk toward the cliffs.

"So what do we do now, boss?" Mr. Data asked.

Dix glanced around at his people. "We spread out and get any information we can find. We're quickly running out of time, people."

All of them nodded.

"Mr. Whelan, I want you to take two others and go see if you can find out where Benny the Banger's headquarters are located. Mr. Data, you and Bev do the same for Harvey Upstairs Benton."

"Don't worry, Boss," Mr. Data said, "we'll sniff him out like a dead skunk, track him like an elephant in mud, seek the—"

Dix held up his hand and Mr. Data stopped. Bev snickered and covered her mouth.

"I'll see if I can locate Slippery Stan Hand's whereabouts," Dix said. "We'll meet back in my office in an hour, no matter what."

"Gotcha, Boss," Mr. Data said, giving him a thumbs-up sign.

"And people," Dix said as two morgue guys wheeled the body of Ghost Johnson past them, strapped down and handcuffed, just in case. "Be careful."

"We only have one problem," Bev said, touching Dix's arm.

"What's that?" Dix said, turning to look into her beautiful, smiling face.

"How do we get back into town?"

Dix glanced out the front door at the dark, windswept night, remembering they had come with Detective Bell in his Dodge. And it didn't seem likely he was going to be leaving any time soon.

"Looks like we're going to have to bum a ride."

"With whom?" Bev asked.

Mr. Data took his mobster stance. "Doll, always remember what Mrs. G— once said. 'In the history of crime and its detection chance plays the chief character.' "

Dixon Hill just shook his head and headed out the door. "Come on, people. Let's go take a chance."

What he didn't say was that they were going to have to be very lucky *and* take a lot of chances to survive for much longer. Somewhere out in this crazy city was a small golden ball that they had to find. He knew the solution to this puzzle was right in front of him.

He just couldn't see it.

Yet.

The life of all his people and this entire city depended on him seeing the obvious, and doing it very soon.

Clues from Dixon Hill's notebook in "The Case of the Missing Heart"

- Ghost Johnson does not have the Heart of the Adjuster, and if he comes back from his death, he will be in jail for a long time to come.
- In this instance, the butler didn't do it, and didn't survive, at least until he comes back as well.
- Attempting to reproduce art only results in poor copies and a critical audience.
- I am convinced that progress has been made in this investigation, even though it feels as if the beginning is at hand again. Suspects have been eliminated.

Chapter Five

There Ain't Nothin' Like a Dame

Section One: She Smells Like a Mystery

DIXON HILL COULD SMELL HER long before he saw her. The clear odor of perfume hung in the hall outside his office like a dark cloud on a horizon, warning of a coming storm. He reached the top of the stairs and took a deep breath. It was as if someone had cut fresh flowers, dipped them in honey, and then run them over a wet dog.

Twice.

The cloying smell hung on everything like moisture after a hot shower. Even the stray cat batting at something at the end of the hallway seemed upset by the smell, and considering that cats love the smell of dead things, that was something.

Dix stared at the door to his outer office, not sure if he should go in or not. He had told his people all to meet here, and he was early. He had had no luck finding out information about Slippery Stan Hand. It was as if no one had heard the name before, or wanted to hear it again.

He squared his shoulders and looked at the door with his name etched in the glass. "Face this like a man," he muttered.

He turned the brass knob and pushed open the door, half surprised the door moved easily through the thick air. Inside the smell was just as bad, but thankfully the room was empty.

For an instant he was sure he could see a lilac-colored cloud in the room, then it vanished. More than likely his imagination, but considering all the strange things happening in this city at the moment, a cloud of perfume in his office might be possible. It certainly *smelled* possible.

He pushed his way through the odor like a salmon swimming upriver, and shoved open his inner office door.

The sight that greeted him set him back on his heels.

A young woman, wearing a tight skirt, a sheer white blouse, and a flowered, wide-brimmed hat, sat on the edge of his desk, smoking a long cigarette in a black holder. With her big brown eyes and long brown hair swept back off her shoulder, she was the most perfectly beautiful image of a woman he had ever seen. And it was clear from every detail of her being that she knew it.

And flaunted it.

From the way she held her cigarette, to the way she

draped her purse over her shoulder, to the skin showing on her crossed legs, she knew the effect her look had on men. Every aspect of this woman was aimed at putting a man off his guard, controlling that man, and getting her way.

For the second time since reaching his office, Dixon Hill squared his shoulders, firmed up his resolve, and pushed the door closed behind him.

He flipped his hat onto the wooden rack, took off his coat and hung it on the stand, and moved toward her.

"You're sitting on my desk."

"I was wondering why I was enjoying it so much," she said, batting her eyes at him, long lashes fluttering in the breeze like torn flags. Her voice was as smooth as glass, not too low, not too high, and very seductive in tone.

Dix moved around behind her, making her turn and slide off the desk to see him. "Well, I have an appointment in a few minutes," Dix said, his voice level and his gaze holding hers, "and I don't appreciate strangers coming into my office and making themselves at home."

"I'm Jessica Daniels," she said, extending a perfectly manicured hand. "I'm hoping we won't be strangers."

He ignored her hand and sat down, pushing his chair back away from his desk and putting his feet up. He needed to be rude to get this woman out of his office and out of his way. There wasn't time for the games this woman would play. Maybe on another day, under different circumstances, he would have enjoyed the sparring, but not today. He had to find the Heart of the Adjuster and find it fast.

"So why come here?" he asked.

She laughed at him, her laugh perfect and refined. "I was told you were a man who got to the point. I see that was an understatement."

"You didn't answer my question," Dix said.

Her lower lip extended and rolled downward as her entire face went into a slight pout. Dix was sure many men would find such an expression hard to resist. To Dix, it only made her look like she had slept on her face on a hard pillow.

He waited until she finished her show, then a few beats longer, letting the tension in the room thicken like a ripe fruit in the hot sun.

Finally she said, "I came to hire you."

"I'm busy on another case," he said. "But thanks for thinking of me."

Again the pout was back, this time with even more effort behind it. Dix had a hard time not laughing at how stupid she looked. For a woman who clearly spent a great deal of time in front of a mirror, she should have known better.

"Why don't you like me?" she asked.

"I didn't say I didn't like you," Dix said. "I don't know you."

"So why are you being so rude?"

"You really want or need an answer to that question?"

She stared at him as she stood in front of his desk. Then she started around the desk.

"Don't even think about it," he said, his voice as low and as cold and as mean as he could make it. He didn't change the position of his hands behind his head, his feet up on the desk, but he didn't need to.

She stopped in her tracks like a deer frozen in a headlight. He could see the stunned look in her eyes behind all the eyeliner. She was clearly confused. She must have never had a man treat her like this before.

She turned to face him, took a deep breath which exaggerated her assets to the fullest degree, then said, "Yes, I would like an answer."

"Don't say I didn't warn you," Dix said.

"I won't," she said.

He let his feet drop to the ground and his chair scoot back, but he didn't stand. "I'm always rude to anyone who thinks they can come into my office and control me. Just a small pet peeve I have."

"What makes you think I wanted to try to control you?" she asked. "I came to hire you."

"I don't think so," Dix said. "I know you want something from me, but I doubt it was to hire me. Otherwise why bathe in too much perfume, wear undergarments meant for ladies of the night, and a dress so tight it leaves nothing to the imagination?"

She opened her mouth and then closed it, like a fish out of water gasping for life. So Dix went on.

"You are a woman who is used to having men fall at your feet and do your bidding. You expected me to do the same."

He looked her up and down, making his motions

large and exaggerated, like a house painter checking to see if he missed anything on a wall.

Then Dix smiled. "And at another time, I might have enjoyed the game and a few dances around the hardwood. But at the moment, as I said, I'm busy. So please take your perfume and your purse and hit the stairs, if you can get down them in those heels."

She blinked twice, and as she did the I'm-a-seductress act dropped off like a coat on a hot day. Her brown eyes turned cold, her face aged right under the makeup, and her posture shifted to one of pity-me defense from complete control.

Dix saw it all, noted it all, but didn't move. He knew any action he could make would be too late.

The small gun appeared from somewhere on her body and she held it pointed at his head as if she knew what she was doing and how to use it. He had no doubt from her posture now that she did.

"Well, Mr. Hill," she said, her voice lower than a moment before and much rougher, as if she had smoked three packs a day for years. "I see that my act was convincing, just not effective."

"The stairs are still behind you, through the two doors," Dix said. He put his feet back up on his desk, his hands behind his head, as if beautiful women pointed small-but-deadly guns at him in his office every day. "But I really would take the shoes off before attempting them."

She laughed, cold and low and rough. "Why are you so anxious to get me out of here?"

"As I said, I have another appointment coming in a few minutes." He looked at her cold eyes and steady hand on the gun. "Besides, your perfume is making me sick to my stomach."

"I could make you a lot sicker," she said, waving the gun sideways to make her point.

"I doubt you're going to do that," he said.

"And why not?"

"You wouldn't get what you came here for."

She studied him for a moment, then laughed again. The gun vanished as quickly as it had appeared, to a location Dix couldn't quite see. Clearly this woman was a pro. She knew her tricks.

"So let's just talk until your appointment arrives," she said. "Would that fit in your schedule?"

"It would seem I have little choice, so go ahead. What would you like me to do for you?"

She moved around the end of the desk and sat on the corner, exposing her smooth legs and giving him an interesting angle looking up at her. He figured she had made the move to make him uncomfortable, so he didn't change position. Behind him, outside the window, the rain had returned, pounding the street below like a drum. It filled the room with a constant background noise.

"I have heard," she said, "that you are looking for Cyrus Redblock. Is that correct?"

"Actually," Dix said, trying not to show his surprise at her question, "I'm looking for a small, gold-colored ball. I just thought Cyrus Redblock, or whoever took him, might be able to help me find it."

She nodded. "What I want you to do is help me find Cyrus."

Now Dix was really surprised.

He lowered himself back to a sitting position, which brought him closer to her legs and her perfume. So he stood and moved away, hands behind his back, as if thinking.

Then he turned back to face her. "Why?"

"I could tell you the reason I had invented for the woman you saw when you came in," she said, smiling at him, her eyes still cold, her expression hard, even as she batted her eyes.

"No, please," Dix said. "Truth."

"I want to kill him," she said.

The harshness and coldness in her words seemed to suck the heat from the room and push back the sounds of the rain like someone had dropped a blanket over everything. Dix was amazed frost didn't form on the inside of the window.

"And then," she said, going on slowly, her voice low and raspy, cutting through the tension in the room like a knife, "I want to make sure he stays dead, even if I have to keep killing him every few hours myself."

"It would get old and tiring, I'm sure," Dix said.

"No, it wouldn't," she said. "I would actually enjoy it, to be honest with you."

He could tell from her eyes that she meant what she said. And that made Dix shiver. This woman was colder and meaner and angrier than he had thought.

They stared at each other for a moment, letting the

cold build. Finally Dix asked. "What did he do to you?"

She smiled, but the smile did nothing to warm the room. "As you said to me, that's a question I don't think you want or need to know."

Dix stared at her for a moment, then decided she was right on that. He didn't need to know. It was clear she hated Cyrus Redblock and wanted him dead. That was more than enough.

"You're right," he said.

"So, can I trust you to tell me when you find him?"

"No," Dix said. "I have no reason to."

Again the gun appeared in her hand like she was a magician pulling cards out of the air. "Is your life, and the lives of your friends, reason enough?"

Dix shrugged. He didn't dare let this woman see a touch of weakness. "It might be, I suppose, if you told me who you were working for."

The gun actually dropped a fraction of an inch, but her expression stayed frozen, as if her makeup had hardened into a false shell. Her working for someone had been an educated guess on his part, but her reaction told him he was right.

"I told you, I want him dead," she said.

"I'm sure you do," Dix said. "I wasn't questioning that. I was asking who you were working for. You be honest with me and I might be tempted to tell you if I find Redblock."

She lowered her arm, but didn't put the gun away this time. Her smile didn't reach her eyes, any more than her phony act when he came in had reached convincing. "I understand, from word on the street, that you were just looking for him."

"Slippery Stan Hand?" Dix said, actually surprised, and not caring if it showed in his voice.

"My boyfriend," she said, her voice soft again. "Stan Hand, the smoothest touch on the west coast."

"So Stan doesn't have Cyrus Redblock, I gather."

She looked at him, her eyes cold, her anger making her almost shake. "No, Redblock had Stan. Took him and killed most of Stan's men yesterday, in a shoot-out."

"Yesterday, before someone took Redblock?" Dix asked, doing his best to make sense of all this new information. Or even believe it.

"Yeah," she said. "And Stan's men ain't doing the walking dead routine. They're starting to smell."

Dix wanted to ask how she could smell anything through her own perfume, but kept his mouth shut.

"So will you help me find Redblock?"

Dix turned and moved away, then stopped and put the information she had given him together. If what she was saying was the truth, then Slippery Stan Hand was eliminated as a possible suspect in the taking of both Redblock and the Heart of the Adjuster. That information would save him some time.

And it wouldn't hurt, if he did find Redblock and got what he needed, to promise to tell this woman Redblock's location. It was a fair trade for the information he had just gotten.

"I'm looking for Redblock, as well as a gizmo he might help me find," Dix said, staring into her cold eyes. "I will tell you when I find him, if you stay out of my way in the process. And if the information you have given me just now is on the level."

"Understood," she said.

The gun in her hand vanished as quickly as it had appeared, and she stepped toward him, smothering him in her honey and flower and wet-dog smell. He couldn't move out of her thankful hug, but there was no doubt he was going to have to change suits after she left. It was going to be questionable if that smell would ever come out.

At that moment, over her shoulder, he saw the door open.

The look on the Luscious Bev's face was not pleasant. Or happy to see him in the embrace of another woman.

*Six hours before
the Heart of the Adjuster is commandeered*

*Captain's Log.
Thirty hours remain until we enter the edge of the* Blackness *and the subspace forces tear the ship apart. Even at this distance from the phenomenon, we are having troubles with many ship's systems. Chief Engineer La Forge has managed to protect environmental controls, but in the last hour, every door to almost every room on the ship opened and stayed frozen open. Except for the*

operation of the lifts, we have ignored the problem.
Privacy is not an issue at the moment. Survival is.

Section Two: He Dances Like He's Named Fred

Dixon Hill pushed the perfume-rich Jessica Daniels to arm's length and then released her like he was dropping a hot potato. He resisted the impulse to try to brush the smell off his jacket and nodded to Bev and Mr. Data. Then he did the two-step side-shuffle to move farther away from her as he did introductions. "This is Ms. Jessica Daniels, girlfriend of Slippery Stan Hand."

Bev gave her a very cold look and said nothing.

Mr. Data went into his mobster stance. "Glad to meet you, toots. What's shakin'?"

"Oh," Jessica said, dropping back into her seductress role like butter melting in a dish, "you're a cute one." She turned away from Dix and moved to Mr. Data.

He stood there, frozen like a white statue as she ran a fingernail along his cheek and along the top of his collar.

"Nice skin," Jessica said, her voice as sickly-sweet as her perfume. "Firm and hard, just the way I like it. But you could use a little sun, doll."

Dix rolled his eyes at Bev, which broke through her shell and made her smile. Then when Jessica wasn't looking, he waved his hand in front of his face, as if trying to fan away the bad smell.

Bev snorted and had to turn her back. She moved to

the window. "Warm in here, isn't it?" she said as she slid the old wooden window upward, letting in the sounds of the rain, the cars on the street, and the city beyond.

The fresh air felt wonderful. Dix took a deep breath. He desperately wanted to go to the window beside Bev and stick his head out, just to try to clear his nose of the cloying smell. But instead he stepped toward Jessica.

"Thanks for stopping by," Dix said, taking Jessica's elbow and trying to move her away from Mr. Data. "I will be in touch the moment I find anything. And I hope you will share information you discover as well."

"Glad to," she said, her voice soft and in the false-sexy mode. She touched Mr. Data's nose with the tip of one finger. "See ya, you big white stud-muffin."

With that she swished out the door, her purse swinging, leaving behind a trail of too many dead flowers.

The three of them stood, saying nothing, until the outer office door closed, then Bev turned to open a second window. "She must bathe in the stuff."

"I might have to have the entire office fumigated," Dix said.

Mr. Data touched his nose where she had tapped him. Clearly he had never had a woman do that before. "Stud-muffin?" he asked.

Dix decided there would be time to explain later. Right now they needed to get on with the task at hand. And that was finding the Heart of the Adjuster.

He was about to ask what Bev and Mr. Data had discovered when a scream echoed through the building.

Then one shot.

It rattled the glass in the door and the concussion seemed to bounce around the room.

Dix knew that shot had been close. Very close. Maybe just outside in the hallway.

Dix was right behind Mr. Data, gun in hand, as they headed through the outer office. When Mr. Data threw open the outer door, the smell of Ms. Daniels' perfume greeted them, along with two other smells.

Gunpowder and blood.

Jessica Daniels lay sprawled on the floor in a very unsexy position, her head tilted against the baseboard, her purse over her head. Blood was smeared down the wall and was flowing from under her body.

She was clearly dead. A simple bullet hole between her eyes made sure of that.

There was no one else to be seen. Even the stray cat that had been haunting the hallway earlier had vanished.

"Check downstairs," Dix ordered. "Whoever did this has to be close."

Mr. Data nodded and dashed down the stairs.

Bev stepped up beside Dix and stood looking at the late Jessica Daniels. "Someone didn't like her talking to you."

Dix nodded. He was thinking the same thing. But there just hadn't been anything she had said to him that had been worth dying for. She had told him her boyfriend, Slippery Stan Hand, had been taken. But nothing beyond that.

The key fact was that someone *thought* she knew something, and had to be stopped.

He glanced at Bev. "Better call Detective Bell. He's going to want to see this before she comes back to life."

"If she comes back to life," Bev said.

Dix only nodded. The way the reality of this city by the bay had been changing, nothing was certain. And that uncertainty was the only sure thing.

> *Four hours before*
> *the Heart of the Adjuster is pirated*

Captain's Log.

Mr. Data and Chief Engineer La Forge have come up with what might be a solution to our problem. Mr. Data's device was intended to adjust screens to match some of the subspace effects pounding us from the four quantum singularities that are forming the Blackness. *But the device can only block a limited and set pattern of such subspace waves. Not enough to allow restarting of the impulse drives.*

The Auriferite that La Forge has been working with also screens out a limited number of such subspace waves, but not enough to allow the restarting of our engines. What they have come up with is a way to project a shield to block almost all of the subspace effects using both Mr. Data's device and the mineral Auriferite.

I have given them permission to test the device first,

*before taking any chance on burning out or destroying
our only supply of Auriferite. For the next two hours
they will run computer simulations, then a final
simulation on the holodeck, before installing the
shielding on the impulse engines. Engineer La Forge
and Mr. Data both assure me the extra few hours will
make no difference in their chance of success.*

Section Three: It Takes a Woman

Dixon Hill waited beside the dead body of Jessica
Daniels as Bev went back into his office to call Detective Bell. A few moments later Mr. Data came back up
the stairs.

"No one in sight, boss," Mr. Data said.

Dix nodded as Bev came back out and stood beside
him. "Detective Bell is on the way."

"Thank you," Dix said.

Bev moved over and kneeled beside the body, avoiding the growing pool of blood. Then she gently picked
up Jessica's purse. The short strap was still clutched in
Jessica's dead fingers, and it took a moment for Bev to
get it free. After she did, she stood and moved back to
Dix and Mr. Data.

"What are you doing?" Mr. Data asked.

"If you want to get to know a woman," Bev said,
"look in her purse."

"Good thinking," Dix said. It was lucky Bev was
here. He would not have come up with that.

Mr. Data glanced at Bev, then at Dix. "Wouldn't you

just ask her questions, or find out where she was from?"

Dix shook his head. "Difficult to do when she's dead."

Mr. Data glanced at the body. "Oh."

"What's the matter, Mr. Data?" Dix asked. "No mystery character quotes for this situation?"

Mr. Data went into his gangster pose. "As Johnny Aysgarth said, 'Circumstances alter women.' " Mr. Data then looked as if he was thinking for a moment before he said, "Actually, Claudio Howard-Wolferstab expressed it better when he said, 'One should never allow one's illusion of woman to be destroyed by a mere accident.' "

Bev smiled at Dix. "Now aren't you sorry you asked?"

"I am, actually," Dix said, holding up his hand for Mr. Data to stop with any more quotes for the moment.

Bev opened the purse and looked inside, holding it slightly sideways to let the light in.

"Let me guess," Dix said. "Perfume?"

"Small bottle," Bev said, picking it out with two fingers and handing it to Mr. Data like it was a snake that might bite.

She kept digging. "A compact," she said, also handing the round item to Mr. Data, who looked almost uncomfortable holding them.

She dug in deeper. "A couple of letters." She handed those to Dix.

He could tell at a glance they were both bills with her address on it. It appeared she lived about six blocks away and closer to the wharf.

"And these," Bev said, holding up a small ring with two keys on it. One looked like a door key, the other some sort of lockbox key.

"Nothing else besides two different lipsticks, a hankie, and a license of some sort," Bev said, shaking the small purse.

She exchanged the keys for the two letters and put them back in, then took the compact and bottle of perfume from Mr. Data and replaced it as well.

"I think we need to pay her apartment a visit," Dix said, swirling the keys on his finger before slipping them into his pocket. Chances are they wouldn't find anything, but it was better to be safe than sorry at this point. He could return her keys to the station later, saying he found them. Detective Bell might raise an eyebrow, but he wouldn't say anything.

Bev nodded, snapped the purse shut and replaced it above Jessica's head, just as footsteps were heard on the stairs.

Mr. Whelan came bounding up the stairs, clearly breathing hard. "Cops parking outside. I got the rest of our people spread out up and down the street, just in case. Anything wrong?"

Then he saw the body and stopped.

"Any information on Benny the Banger?" Dix asked as the sounds of the door opening downstairs filled the stairway.

"Nothing," Mr. Whelan said. "Not a clue where his headquarters might be."

"Then for the moment, she's our only lead," Dix said, nodding at the dead woman.

"I'm almost afraid to ask what happened," Mr. Whelan said.

"So am I," Detective Bell said as he rounded the corner of the stairs and climbed up to them. He stood staring at the woman for a moment, then turned to Dix. "People are ending up dead around you a lot lately."

"Ghost Johnson still in that state?" Dix asked.

"Nope," Bell said, "Came back to life in handcuffs and facing a long stretch of jail time just before I got this call."

Bell moved over and looked closer at the woman. "What did she do? Fall on a bottle of perfume?"

He waved a hand in front of his face as if that would help get rid of the smell, then he knelt down over her. A moment later he glanced back at Dix with a surprised look on his face. "This wouldn't happen to be Jessica Daniels, would it? Slippery Stan Hand's best girl?"

"The one and the same," Dix said.

"Oh, just peachy," Bell said, standing and moving back to face Dix. "You got any idea what this is going to stir up?"

"I have a hunch," Dix said. "And I didn't do it, just for the record."

"And, I suppose," Detective Bell said, "you didn't see who did?"

"Nope," Dix said. "We were inside my office, with both doors closed when we heard the shot."

"I checked downstairs a few moments afterward," Mr. Data said. "There were no suspicious characters in sight."

"Thanks," Bell said, staring at Jessica's body. "I guess."

"If the second chance at life is still working," Dix said, "you can wait a few hours and just ask her who did it."

Detective Bell nodded. "And if she doesn't do the resurrection bit, and I don't do this crime scene right, my head will be on a platter."

Dix knew exactly what he meant. There was no depending on anything at this point. It was better to stay with the old methods that were proven to work. And for him, that meant good old-fashioned detective work.

"So any idea why someone did this?" Bell asked, staring at Dix. "Like what she was doing here, outside your office?"

"She wanted to hire me," Dix said. "To find her boyfriend."

"Find him?" Bell asked, stunned. "When did *he* go missin'?"

"When Cyrus Redblock snatched him," Dix said, telling Bell what he knew from Jessica, "right before someone snatched Redblock. And Jessica presumed her boyfriend as well."

"This is givin' me a headache," Bell said.

Dix could only agree. Someone shooting her just

didn't make sense. At least not yet. But there was clearly a lot Dixon Hill didn't know about what was happening in the city.

Ten minutes later they had given Bell and the other cops their statements and were headed down the stairs for Jessica Daniels' apartment. There weren't many hours left before this world and everything around it came to a sudden end. Dixon Hill was starting to feel the pressure of every lost minute. Somehow, some way, they had to find the Heart of the Adjuster.

But in a big city, finding something no larger than a child's ball was going to be hard. And doing it with no real leads, and only hours left, seemed impossible.

Dixon Hill, Bev, Mr. Data, and Whelan reached the street and stepped into the cold, hard rain. The darkness and the wet didn't help his mood.

Clues from Dixon Hill's notebook in "The Case of the Missing Heart"

- Cyrus Redblock kidnapped Slippery Stan Hand before he was snatched himself.
- Benny the Banger is going to be hard to find.
- Jessica Daniels was killed, more than likely by someone who thought she had information she shouldn't be spreading around.

Chapter Six

Something Smells Like A
Red Herring

Section One: A Woman's Home is Her Mess

Dixon Hill glanced back through the rain at the group following him down the sidewalk toward Jessica Daniels' apartment. Bev and Mr. Data were right behind him, then Whelan and the four others who had offered to help. They all knew something about this city. But eight was too many people to go directly into the apartment at once. They would all be tripping over each other like a crowd trying to climb on a bus. Dix waited until they were two blocks from their destination before holding up his hand for everyone to stop and gather around him on the sidewalk.

The three- and four-story buildings on both sides of the street were dark, full of people sleeping through this seemingly perpetual night. Cars were parked along the curb, landmarks to a time of daylight and movement. Nothing stirred on this cold, wet side street except a stray cat that ran down the gutter and then ducked into a side alley. In the distance a dog barked, then stopped, followed by a distant siren that quickly faded.

As everyone stopped moving the street's silence pounded into Dix like a hammer, taking his breath away with the idea that soon everything would be silenced in a much more permanent fashion if he didn't succeed in this search. He could feel the weight on his shoulders, pressing him down into the concrete.

Bev noticed the oppressive silence as well, looking around, clearly not comfortable. "I never knew a city could be so deathly still."

"Maybe this isn't normal," Dix said, his voice a whisper just loud enough for Bev to hear. "Maybe the reality is shifting again."

Bev said nothing, letting the silence rule.

The rain had slacked off just after they left the office and then stopped a block or so back, but it had already done its damage to all of them. Dix was wet and chilled. Bev's hair was flat on her head, and all their coats were soaked through.

Dix waited until everyone was gathered around closely so he didn't have to speak loudly, as if he was in a funeral home and afraid to wake the dead. Even trying to keep his words soft, his words seemed louder than they needed to be. "Mr. Whelan, I want you to take your people and spread out along the street, taking up positions at both intersections on either side of Ms. Daniels' apartment and around behind as well."

"Got it," Whelan said.

"And be careful," Dix said. "Someone killed Jessica Daniels for a reason. That person may be watching her apartment. I want to know at once if you see anything suspicious."

Whelan nodded and turned, indicating the four others should follow him.

Dix, Bev, and Mr. Data waited until the sounds of footsteps had died off against the black windows. Then Dix took Jessica Daniels' apartment keys out of his pocket and jingled them, the noise clear in the cold night air. "Let's go."

"Right behind ya, boss," Mr. Data said.

To Dix it seemed an eternity to walk the two blocks, their heels clicking on the blackened concrete, every window a dead eye staring down on them. The air between the buildings didn't seem to move and Dix wished for a wind or even the slightest breeze to break the oppressive stillness.

Nothing.

Only the sounds of their steps and the heavy silence of the city traveled with them to the building listed on Jessica Daniels' bills. It looked like any of the other three-story buildings along the street, with concrete steps up to a wide entrance. Dix knew that her apartment was on the second floor. There were no lights in any of the windows.

"We go in slow and carefully," Dix said, indicating Mr. Data should lead.

Gun in hand, Mr. Data started up, moving like a cat, slowly, cautiously.

The front door of the building had a slight squeak that echoed down the street, and the wooden stairs just inside the second door creaked far too loudly under all their weight.

They had no choice but to keep moving.

The second floor landing was lit with a single, faint bulb hanging from a cord. The stairs going up to the third floor seemed to disappear into blackness.

There were two wooden doors, Jessica's on the right with the number 202 in brass.

As quietly as he could, Dix unlocked the door with her key and then, indicating that Mr. Data and Bev should stand back, he swung the door open, staying out of the line of fire from anyone who might be inside.

Silence and darkness greeted them.

And perfume. A wave of it covered them, flowing out of the apartment like water released from a dam.

Dix held his breath and remained still for a five count.

Nothing.

Mr. Data shook his head meaning that he could hear nothing inside.

Dix nodded, then indicated he would go in first.

Slowly, staying low, Dix eased through the door into the thick smell and felt for a switch on the wall. It was where it should be and the lights blinded him for a moment as he flipped them on with a sharp click.

"Wow," Bev said when it became clear there was no one inside, "she didn't believe in straightening up."

"I think she had some help in making the mess," Dix said, glancing around at the clutter that filled Jessica Daniels' apartment.

Someone had done a search just recently, and not a neat search. Jessica's clothes were pulled out of the closet and scattered on the floor, her furniture, including a large couch and love seat, had been turned over, and her bed in a second open room had been pulled apart. The entire place reeked of her perfume, as if it had covered everything and the search had shaken it loose.

"Whoever did this," Bev said, "clearly thinks Jessica has something of value to hide."

"Maybe it's the Heart, boss," Data said.

"Well, let's look around," Dix said, easing the apartment door closed. "Maybe they missed whatever it was they were searching for."

"Do you have to close the door?" Bev asked, waving a hand in front of her face. "We might die of perfume poisoning before we finish this."

He didn't move to open the door.

"A window then?"

Dix shook his head. "Just search and we can get out of here."

Bev shook her head and turned to work.

Dix honestly didn't believe Jessica Daniels had the Heart of the Adjuster, or that it was still in this apartment if she somehow had managed to get her hands on it. But there might be a clue here to give them another place to go.

Another lead.

Anything to find out who was behind all of the abductions and killings. And who had what Dixon Hill needed to save everything, and everyone.

> *Two hours before*
> *the Heart of the Adjuster is ripped off*

Captain's Log.

I have given, with great hesitation, Mr. Data and Chief Engineer La Forge permission to set up a test of the device they are calling the Adjuster on the holodeck. Due to the subspace distortions coming from the four singularities forming the Blackness, *all ship's systems are unstable, the holodeck among them. I have been informed that it has flashed through ten different programs in the last hour, including two Klingon training scenarios and a Dixon Hill case. The safety devices in the holodeck are going off and on like a flashing light.*

Chief Engineer La Forge has assured me that he will set up a screen using a small portion of the Auriferite mineral around the controlling systems of the holodeck to make sure the holodeck functions within a safe range. He tells me there may still be some fluctuations, but not enough to make a difference in their tests.

I am not assured, since the mineral does not screen a large percentage of the subspace disturbances. My officers both feel they need to adjust their device

*before a full-scale attempt is made to shield the
impulse engines and restart them. Otherwise they risk
the entire device and all the mineral needed to make it
work.*

*They have assured me that the only way is to set up a
test on the holodeck. They feel the risk of losing the
device in the holodeck is worth the greater risk of not
having a test and failing on the restart of the impulse
engines. So I have reluctantly agreed.*

*I am continuing to keep other personnel following
other possible means of solving our problem, but so far
this device is our most promising lead.*

Section Two: I Wouldn't Go Down There

With Dixon Hill, Mr. Data, and Bev all searching
Jessica Daniels' apartment, the mess just got worse. If
poor Jessica did recover from her sudden death, she
was going to find an apartment that would take some
time to make livable again. Normally Dix would have
cared, but if they didn't find the Heart of the Adjuster
soon, Jessica and the rest of them would have no home
to come back to. So at the moment he was beyond wor-
rying about being neat.

"Dix," Bev called out. "Take a look at these."

Dix moved over to where she stood by an end table.
There was a big glass ashtray on the ground and scat-
tered around it were a dozen or so books of matches.
The matchbooks all had writing on them.

She handed one to Dix.

Printed clearly on the pack was "Hand's Garage and Service."

There was an address on it that was only about three blocks away. He glanced at Bev. "Seems to me like you found the address of Slippery Stan Hand's business."

"Would seem that way," Bev said, giving him her best smile. Even after walking in the rain, she still looked great as far as Dix was concerned. After this was all over, he owed her a big dinner and a night on the town.

"Boss," Mr. Data called out from across the room. "Come and give a gander at dis."

Dix pocketed the book of matches and he and Bev moved to where Mr. Data stood behind an overturned love seat.

"What did you find?" Dix asked.

Mr. Data pointed at the lower edge of the love seat.

At first Dix could see nothing out of the ordinary. The bottom of the piece of furniture had four wooden legs and was covered with a burlap-type cloth. There was some manufacturing writing on the cloth, but nothing else.

Then, just as he was going to ask Mr. Data what he was pointing at, Dix saw along the seam on the back side of the chair a flap of cloth. He reached down and eased the flap back to expose a zipper.

"The bottom of a chair with a zipper in it?" Bev asked. "That makes no sense."

Dix had to agree. A zipper wasn't something any

normal manufacturer would put in a bottom of a chair, and it was so hidden as to be overlooked by the person who did the first search.

Dix slowly opened the zipper and exposed a large, black notebook. He pulled it out, made sure there was nothing else in the hidden pocket, then stood and opened the book.

Handwritten dates, times, and money amounts greeted him. It took Dix a moment of study and flipping through the book to understand what he was holding. This book was full of detailed records of bribes to cops and city officials, hundreds of them, at all levels.

Bribes by Cyrus Redblock.

But what was it doing hidden in the couch of the girlfriend of Slippery Stan Hand?

Suddenly Dix understood part of what had gone on.

Somehow Slippery Stan Hand copped this book from Cyrus Redblock. That must have really taken some planning and guts.

But then Redblock discovered who had taken it, and went and put the snatch on Hand, killing his men and taking him, but not finding the book, because Hand had hidden the book here. No wonder this apartment had been searched.

That still didn't answer the question of who then snatched Redblock.

Or who had the Heart.

"Amazing," Bev said, looking over Dix's right shoulder. "Whoever controlled this book would control the city."

"I would imagine it was how Redblock kept such a tight hold on everything for so long," Dix said.

Mr. Data went into his tough-guy stance. "As O'Mallery said, 'A guy slips a cop a ten-dollar bill they call it a bribe, but a waiter just takes it and says thank you.' "

"I think the money in the bribe is for a different service," Bev said.

Mr. Data just shrugged. "I just quote 'em, toots."

Dix did a quick flip-through to make sure his friend Detective Bell wasn't on the take, then closed the book. Dix was glad to see he wasn't. At least not from Cyrus Redblock.

Dix patted the book. "Now we've got something to bargain with."

"Bargain with?" Bev asked.

Dix stashed the book inside his raincoat by slipping the book into the top of his pants against the small of his back. His belt would hold it in place and no one would be able to see it under his jacket and raincoat.

"Sure," he said. "Someone has the Heart, we have Cyrus Redblock's bribe record book. Fair trade."

"You'd give that book to someone besides the police?" Bev asked. She looked almost stunned.

"I'd give a lot more than the book in exchange for the Heart right now."

Bev stared at him for a moment, then nodded. "Good point. So to Stan's headquarters next?"

"You got it in one," Dix said. He pulled out the keys to Jessica's apartment. "Unless you might have any idea what this small key goes to."

The all stared at the small lockbox key as both Bev and Mr. Data shook their heads.

"Nothing anywhere in here that comes close?" Dix asked, and got the same response.

"All right, let's go." Dix led the way out of the apartment, making sure to lock the door behind them as they went.

"Ah, fresh air," Bev said, taking a deep breath as they went down onto the street.

Dix did the same, but he knew the smell and taste of Jessica Daniels' perfume was going to be with him for a long, long time.

Ten minutes later, Mr. Whelan and the others had set up watch posts around Stan Hand's garage, while Mr. Data and Bev followed Dix to the business.

It looked like any other car garage in the city, filling a corner of a city block. It was one story tall with a lone gas pump sitting out near the curb, making it look like a stubby cousin to all the taller apartment buildings around it.

Dix walked up and looked through the grease-covered window of the garage. Bev did the same to the office window. A few cars were up on lifts inside the garage, and tools were scattered on the floor. No sign of anyone, or any bodies.

"No one in the office," Bev said, staring in a window on the side of the shop.

A CLOSED sign had been stuck in the window. Dix moved over and looked in beside her. He could see a desk covered with papers and a trash basket overflowing on the floor. A few car keys hung on hooks on the wall.

To Dix it looked as if someone had just closed up for the night.

"Boss, take a look here," Mr. Data said.

He was pointing at a few slips of paper tacked to the office door.

Dix moved over and glanced at them without taking any of them down. They were from unhappy customers who had left cars here and wanted to pick them up, and were not happy the garage was closed. Clearly this business had not been open for a period of time.

"Time to take a look inside," Dix said.

Mr. Data tried the front door. Locked.

"This way," Dix said, leading the way around to the back. One side was a three-story apartment building, much like the one that Jessica Daniels had lived in. A small wooden fence split the area between the two buildings. They made their way between some barrels filled with oil and the block garage building. The back door was locked as well, but Mr. Data put his shoulder into it and the old wood broke open like it was tissue.

The inside was much warmer than outside and smelled of gas and oil mixed with rotting flesh. Suddenly Jessica Daniels' perfume seemed almost inviting.

"Oh, this isn't going to be fun," Bev said, waving her hand in front of her face.

Dix could only agree. But they had no choice.

"This way," he said, following the stink past the cars on the lifts and into a side office behind the main office. There, an open door led to a staircase leading downward. More than likely that had been the entrance to Slippery Stan Hand's headquarters. The reek of death coming from that door completely covered the oil and gasoline smell from the garage.

"Jessica said Stan's gang was starting to smell," Dix said, putting his coat sleeve over his nose to help block the odor. "She wasn't kidding."

Dix flipped a switch at the top of the stairs, exposing the room below. One man's body lay at the foot of the stairs, as if tossed there. Dix could see others beyond, swarming with flies. It was a scene out of a bad horror movie, with dried brown blood, swarming maggots, and all.

Dix tried to imagine Cyrus Redblock and his men fighting their way in here and doing this. It was possible, but it had to have been risky. Of course, if Slippery Stan Hand had been the one to take the book pressed against the small of Dix's back, Redblock had had no choice. This killing made sense under those conditions in Redblock and Slippery Stan Hand's world. But Redblock, in this raid, hadn't found the book because Slippery Stan had hidden it in a chair in his girlfriend's apartment.

Which was why Redblock had taken Stan Hand alive. All this made sense to Dix.

"I think we could use a few bottles of Jessica's perfume right about now," Bev said.

"I'm not bothered by the smell, boss," Mr. Data said. "You want me to go search the place?"

Dix looked at the empty eyes of the dead man below him and decided he and Bev would be of no real service down there.

"Yes, please," Dix said, "and make sure you don't miss anything. Especially a metal lockbox that Jessica's small key might fit into."

"Gotcha," Mr. Data said, moving down the stairs and into the midst of the stinking bodies.

Dix watched him descend into the man-made hell, then he and Bev retreated through the office and out the back door into the wonderful, clear, and damp air of the city night.

Between Jessica's perfume, the smell coming from that basement, and not finding the Heart of the Adjuster, this night had really stunk.

And there were no signs of it being over yet.

Thirty minutes before
the Heart of the Adjuster is removed

Captain's Log.
Mr. Data and Chief Engineer La Forge are almost finished with their holodeck tests. Twice the holodeck program flickered, but quickly returned to the program they were using. For the past hour the doors to the holodeck have been stuck open as well. Otherwise, I have been told, the tests are going as well as my two officers had hoped. They will run one more test, then install the

device near the impulse engines. We have just over twenty-four hours before this ship enters the Blackness. *For my peace of mind, we are cutting this far too closely.*

Section Three: Another Bargaining Chip

Dix and Bev waited, standing near the corner of the garage, looking out onto the dark, silent street corner. The air was still and cold, almost biting. Dix could see his breath in front of his face again.

He started to pace, then forced himself to stop and remain silent, just in case anyone was coming at them. Dix knew that two of his people were hidden in doorways down the street, but he couldn't even spot them.

Bev fidgeted as the waiting seemed to grow in length. To Dix if felt as if nothing existed at the moment except him and Bev and the cold, dark street corner.

"How long has it been?" Bev finally asked, breaking the silence of the night with a whisper.

"He's doing a thorough search," Dix said. "Give him a few more minutes."

Bev sighed, her breath a white cloud vanishing in the air in front of her face.

Finally, Mr. Data stepped from the back door of the garage and headed toward them carrying a small metal box. He stopped a normal distance in front of Dix, but the smell of death and rotting human flesh he carried with him didn't. It smacked into Dix's face and nose like a hard slap, sending him a step backward.

"Oh, my," Bev said, as she too stepped backward.

"Boss?" Mr. Data asked, stepping closer. "What's wrong?"

Again Mr. Data's sickly smell crashed into Dix's senses, made worse by the contrast of the clear night air around them. Dix felt his stomach twist and he forced himself to swallow.

Again Dix and Bev both stepped back, closer to the street.

Mr. Data was about to come closer again, chasing them with his unseen weapon, when Dix held up his hand. "Stay where you are, Mr. Data," he said. "Tell us what you found."

Mr. Data looked puzzled for a moment, then nodded. "I found ten bodies. The room had been searched. None of the men carried the Heart of the Adjuster, but I did find this, hidden behind a loose stone block in the wall."

Mr. Data held out the metal box.

"How did you find it when whoever killed those men didn't?" Bev asked.

"My question exactly," Dix said. "Was it obvious?"

"No," Mr. Data said. "But I felt there had to be a hiding place of some sort down there. And the back wall made of stone seemed like a logical place." Mr. Data went into his gangster pose. "As Merle Weir once said, 'There's more in most things than meets the eye.' "

"No kidding," Dix said, putting a hand over his nose. He took a deep breath and held it, then stepped toward Mr. Data and took the box, stepping back quickly while indicating Mr. Data should not move. It still wasn't fast enough to escape the awful smell Mr. Data carried with him from that basement.

Dix fished Jessica Daniels' keys out of his pocket and tried the small one on the box. As he suspected it might, the key fit and opened the box.

Inside there was a stack of money and another ledger. Dix opened the ledger. Right up front were the addresses of every major crime lord in the city, plus a few he hadn't heard about. It seemed he now knew where the headquarters of Benny the Banger and Harvey Upstairs Benton were. Benny's was only ten blocks away, pretty close to the spot where Benny's goon had tried to stop him on the street.

Dix flipped through the rest of the book. It was the same sort of thing that Cyrus Redblock had done in his ledger. Mostly it was records of payoffs to cops and others. Again Dix did a quick check to make sure Detective Bell wasn't in the book. Dix was happy to see he wasn't.

Now they had a lot more to trade, if they could just find someone to trade with.

Dix handed the book to Bev. "Hide this on you somewhere," he said.

She nodded and a moment later the book disappeared under her coat.

Dix made sure there was nothing else besides the money in the box, then locked it again and tossed it to Mr. Data. "Put that back in the wall, but make sure you leave the rock out just enough so someone with a good eye will find it."

"Gotcha, boss," Mr. Data said, turning to head back into the garage.

"And Mr. Data," Dix said, "when you are finished, find Detective Bell and report finding the bodies, nothing more. Don't tell him about us being here, or finding any ledgers."

Mr. Data nodded.

"And one more thing," Dix said. "Before you rejoin us, change clothes and wash off."

"Boss?" Mr. Data asked, clearly puzzled.

"Trust him," Bev said. "I'd toss that suit away if I were you."

Mr. Data looked down at his suit as if searching for a hole.

"Meet us at Benny the Banger's headquarters when you are finished," Dix said. He gave Mr. Data the address and then turned to head off down the street, motioning for Mr. Whelan to gather up his men and follow.

"Now what are we going to do?" Bev asked, walking beside him, her breath white in the cold night air.

"What can we do?" Dix asked. "We're going to keep following this trail until it goes dead, or someone drags a red herring across our path."

"You sure after the perfume and the odor of those bodies, we'd smell it if they did?" Bev asked, laughing.

"After what we've been through tonight," Dix said, "I don't think my nose will ever work right again. And it feels as if we've been going in the wrong direction right from the start."

He had had that nagging feeling for some time, but saying it out loud made it even stronger.

"I've had the same feeling," Bev said.

They walked for a half block, saying nothing, their heels clicking on the sidewalk, the sound of the other men following in the distance.

Finally Bev said what Dix had been thinking. "The problem is, I don't see any other direction."

"Neither do I," Dix said. "So no matter how much it stinks, we follow it."

Clues from Dixon Hill's notebook in "The Case of the Missing Heart"

- Cyrus Redblock's ledger of bribes to cops and city officials would be enough to control the city.
- Slippery Stan Hand had somehow taken the book and stashed it in Jessica Daniels' apartment.
- Slippery Stan Hand had his own ledger of bribes.

Chapter Seven

Who Was That Masked Man?

Section One: Only a Shadow

LOTS OF ELEMENTS make people see things that aren't there on a city street late at night. Shadows of the cars parked along the street, the blackness of the alleys, the shades of gray tempered only by a distant streetlight. With the Luscious Bev beside him, and five of his men a short distance behind, Dixon Hill walked purposely through one of the darkest areas of the city. The buildings were in poor repair, garbage littered the street and sidewalk, and the lights on each corner had long ago burnt out and not been replaced.

Behind every car he thought he saw something move.

Beyond every corner a gunman shifted.

Down every side alley a figure ran.

His imagination was taking every shadow, every dark shape, and turning it into an enemy. He kept trying to tell himself he was seeing things. There couldn't be a group of men following them so carefully.

That's what he kept repeating to himself every time another motion caught the edge of his vision, but it didn't help. He kept seeing things.

Finally, a shadow seemed to form into the shape of a man fifty paces in front of them, then slide off into an alley.

"Did you see that?" Bev whispered as she matched him stride-for-stride down the sidewalk.

"You saw it as well?" Dix asked, stunned.

"I've been seeing things in the shadows since we left the garage," Bev said. "I'm spooked by it, let me tell you."

"I thought I was imagining it all," Dix said. "We can't both be imagining the same things, now can we?"

"Not likely," Bev said. "But considering the condition of the reality we find ourselves in, and what is happening in this city, anything is possible."

Dix had to agree with that. But at least he hadn't been imagining things. And if these shapes were real, they could be caught.

At that moment a cat yowled and streaked across the street in front of them. It was being chased by a large dog into an alley. Dix followed the cat and dog with his gaze, only to see another shadowy figure lurking in the darkness. This shadow seemed to be wearing a trench coat and hat.

"There's no doubt we're being tailed," Dix whispered to Bev, "by a group that is doing its best to stay out of our way."

Dix touched Bev's arm just enough to keep her with him as he slowed his pace, letting Mr. Whelan and the rest catch up. When they were only a few paces behind, Dix motioned for Mr. Whelan to come up beside him.

"See the men shadowing us?" Whelan asked. "They are pretty darned good at it."

"Not good enough to keep us from seeing them," Dix said.

"Maybe they want us to see them," Bev said.

Dix thought that over. There was a chance of that, but more than likely the men shadowing them worked for one of the crime bosses. Maybe, if Dix was lucky, the one who had the Heart of the Adjuster.

"Okay, we're going to call their bluff," Dix whispered to Bev and Mr. Whelan. "They want to play cat and mouse, we'll give them a little confusion to go along with the mix. Have everyone stay ready, hands on their guns."

Whelan nodded.

"And stay within ten paces of us," Dix said. "I don't want to go spreading out too much. And follow my lead."

"Understood," Mr. Whelan said, slowing down and dropping back to the men behind. Dix could barely hear him whispering the instructions to the others. He gave Mr. Whelan enough time, then again with his arm against Bev's arm, he increased their pace.

Quickly, he moved their speed up to a point where Bev was almost having to break into a trot to keep up. Dix could hear that behind him the other men were matching the speed.

They reached a corner and Dix turned right, moving at the same speed for the entire length of the city block.

The shadows around them seemed to be a little more obvious, a little more rushed to find cover ahead of them.

At the next corner, Dix again turned right, heading back in the direction they had come from a few moments before, only one block over.

That move caught one of their trailing friends actually out in the middle of the street. He wore a dark coat with the collar up and a dark hat, showing almost no face. He moved quickly into an alley between two buildings as they marched past. Dixon Hill ignored him.

At the next corner they turned right again.

Dix could feel himself starting to breath hard, and Bev was clearly having trouble maintaining the pace in the high-heeled fashion of the day.

One more right at the next corner and they had gone completely around the block. This move again caught a man in a dark coat out in the open. The guy shook his head and ducked for cover.

At the next corner, Dix turned his group right again, covering the same ground they had already covered. But this time, not more than twenty paces down the sidewalk, Dix grabbed Bev's arm, stopped quickly, and turned around, heading back in the direction they had just come at the same fast walk.

They went right through the startled group with Mr. Whelan and back around the corner, this time to the left, retracing their steps.

The guy who had ducked for cover a moment before was back out in the open. And close to the corner, clearly moving to try to follow them.

Dix pulled out his gun and leveled it on the guy. "You move and you're going to be testing the rebirth theory."

The guy froze like a deer in the headlights of a Ford.

Dix motioned for Mr. Whelan and the others to take up positions along the street in the shadows, guarding both ends of the block. He motioned Bev to go with them. Then Dix moved up to the man he had captured in the middle of the street and took his gun, tucking it away.

"What do you say we just stand here," Dix said, "until your friends come out of hiding?"

The guy, his eyes dark slits under his hat, said nothing.

It didn't take long, as Dix figured it wouldn't. Another man in a dark coat came around the corner at a run. He stopped cold when he saw Dix and his prisoner in the middle of the road.

Mr. Whelan stepped out of a shadow, gun drawn. "Hands in the air, or I put you face down in the gutter."

The man froze for an instant, then raised his hands.

Dix motioned for Mr. Whelan to bring him to the center of the street.

"I figure you have two more friends out there yet," Dix said.

At that moment, from the other direction, another man came around the corner, running, his coat flapping. He too was quickly captured.

Dix and Mr. Whelan moved all three prisoners out of the street and over to the mouth of an alleyway and back into the darkness.

"What do you plan on doin' with us?" the man Dix had captured asked.

"Shadows speak," Dix said. "I'm stunned."

At that moment one more dark-coated man appeared at a run and found himself facing two of Dix's men, guns drawn.

"I'm betting that's all of you," Dix said. "You want to tell me different?"

The guy said nothing.

"Cat got your tongue?" Dix asked. He motioned to Mr. Whelan. "Line them up against the wall."

The alley was just dark enough to make everyone look like a dark shadow, yet light enough to see what they were doing. Dix was counting on the darkness to help his plan, just as these four had used the same darkness to follow them.

Whelan and the others did as they were told, then Dix had everyone stand back. Dix turned to his people and in such a fashion that the men against the wall couldn't see, winked at Whelan and Bev. "Follow my lead," he whispered.

Whelan and the man next to him nodded.

Dix turned back to their prisoners. "I'll take the one on the far right," Dix said. "Each of you take one and we'll get this over with and get on our way."

"I got the one next in line," Mr. Whelan said.

Two other men added they would take care of the other two.

"Make your shots count," Dix said. "Clean shots between the eyes. No point in making them suffer."

"How about we use their own guns," Mr. Whelan said, extending the charade.

"Good idea," Dix said, taking from his belt the gun he had taken from the man in the street.

"Give me a second, Dix," Bev said, moving toward the sidewalk at the mouth of the dark alley. "I don't want to get blood on my shoes like the last time."

"Wait!" the man Dix had first caught shouted, his voice echoing in the narrow, dark alleyway, the panic clear. "You can't just go an' kill us."

"And why not?" Dix asked. "Wasn't that what you had intended for us?"

"No," the guy said, his head shaking as if someone was yanking it with a rope. "We was supposed ta just follow ya."

"And who gave you that order?" Dix asked.

"Benny da Banger," the guy said, glancing at the man beside him against the wall, who seemed just fine with giving up information in exchange for not being killed.

"Well, isn't that a surprise," Dix said. "We were just on our way to visit him."

The guy said nothing.

"Well," Dix said, "the way I figure it, we take out you four here, we have less to deal with when we get to your boss."

"He don't want a fight with ya," the man said.

"Then why did he want you to follow us?" Dix asked, waving the man's gun in his face.

The guy was breathing so hard, he was almost panting. He glanced at the other men beside him. All seemed to be staring ahead in the darkness, looking at the guns aimed at them. None of them were going to give him any help, that much was clear.

"He just wanted to make sure of somethin'," the guy said.

"And just what would that something be?" Dix asked.

Again the guy hesitated, then blurted out the answer. "That you wasn't da one who took out Stan Hand and Redblock's gangs. Benny figured since you and da cop took down da Undertaker and Ghost Johnson, you might be gunnin' for him next."

"And what if I was gunning for Benny?" Dix asked. "What were your orders then?"

The guy swallowed so hard, the gulp echoed off the brick walls.

"You were supposed to stop us, right?" Dix asked.

The guy said nothing.

"So why shouldn't we just stop you here and now?" Dix asked, his voice as low and as mean as he could make it. "Seems only fair to me." He raised his gun.

"Yeah, me too," Whelan said, following Dix's example.

"Wait!" the guy shouted, holding up his hands and waving them. "I told ya everythin'!"

"Really?" Dix asked. "You didn't tell me who *did* snatch Redblock."

"The boss thinks it was Upstairs Benton."

"And you think for your lives, your boss might be willing to work with me in finding Benton?"

The guy looked like he might be sick. His eyes were large, filled with fear. Dix knew without a doubt he was telling the truth.

"I don't know," he said. "I can't be speakin' for Benny. He'd kill me quicker den you can."

"Now I know I'm getting the truth," Dix said, lowering his gun. "How about we all go for a little walk to talk to Benny, as if we're all the best of friends?"

Dix put the gun back in his belt and motioned for the others to do the same.

Benny's men slowly lowered their hands, clearly confused.

"This way, I think," Dix said, motioning for the men to head back out of the alley and into the street with him. "Unless I got my address wrong."

The guy nodded and stepped away from the wall, moving up to a spot beside Dix as they walked down the middle of the street.

The silence of the night was broken by the heels on pavement of the small parade all marching toward the same destination.

Dix let everyone walk in silence for a block, then turned to Benny's man beside him. "I'm really not looking to take down Benny," Dix said. "Just looking for a small gold-painted ball about this size." Dix held up his finger and thumb to show the man how big the Heart of the Adjuster was. "You seen anything like it?"

The guy shook his head. "Naw, nothin' like that."

Dix could feel the disappointment and the slight feeling of panic twist through his stomach. They had to find the Heart quickly. It was only a matter of three or four hours now. And if this guy was telling the truth, then it was Harvey Upstairs Benton that might have it.

Unless he had been following the wrong lead the entire time. What happened if Harvey had snatched Redblock and Slippery Stan Hand, but hadn't taken the Heart? That would leave them at square zero with no time left. But someone had taken the Heart out of the Adjuster, someone in this world, some thief with connections to Redblock or one of the other bosses and this entire mess.

So right now, they had one suspect left, and the only choice was to follow that one lead until they found the Heart or ran out of time.

Or came up with a better idea.

Right now, in the middle of the dark street, with people following him like the Pied Piper, Dixon Hill was fresh out of ideas.

> *Thirty-seven minutes after*
> *the Heart of the Adjuster is stolen*

Captain's Log. Personal.

A short time ago, while Chief Engineer La Forge and Mr. Data were finishing the last of their tests on a device to shield the impulse drives from the effects of the Blackness, the holodeck malfunctioned and switched to the Dixon Hill program. The device they were working on was unharmed, but on the switch, two things happened that led to what may be a fatal series of events.

First, the safety features of the holodeck were shut off by the malfunction, leaving Mr. Data and Engineer La Forge in that world, standing over a small device they were calling the Adjuster.

They were located just outside the office of the fictional character, Dixon Hill, near the top of the stairs. However, they could not leave, since the malfunction also closed and locked the holodeck doors.

Both men moved to find a way to reopen the doors, while other members of the crew worked from the outside toward the same aim.

During their attempts the Dixon Hill program switched three times, once leaving them standing in the middle of a busy street for ten seconds, a second time moving them to the sidewalk for almost a minute, but always bringing them back to the hallway outside Dixon Hill's office.

After ten minutes of work on both sides of the door, the malfunction was corrected and the door opened. At that point, when Engineer La Forge turned to retrieve the Adjuster, it was discovered that the small golden ball of the material Auriferite was missing.

There are no sides on the Adjuster, and the Auriferite was simply sitting on a small platform in the center, easily taken while the men worked on the doors.

The staircase to that floor of the building was where Mr. Data and Chief Engineer La Forge could not see anyone coming up or down. And anyone seeing that device sitting there would instantly want the gold ball inside it, since it looks valuable.

Both men assure me that without that small ball of Auriferite, the Adjuster will not work. It is somewhere in the program for Dixon Hill, and if the program is shut down, it will be lost into the holographic matrix, just as sure as if someone had transported it into space.

La Forge and everyone with any knowledge or wild idea are continuing to work on the problem of shielding the impulse engines from the effects of the Blackness. *It seems my only choice is to take as many people as possible into the world of Dixon Hill and work to find the ball.*

Mr. Data, using a small portion of the remaining Auriferite, has put up a shield around the main controls of the holodeck to keep it from shutting down, but it cannot be changed. The world of Dixon Hill is very much alive and working in there, and the safeties are off, which will make it a very deadly place.

But there is no choice. The golden ball of Auriferite is in there somewhere, taken by someone. It can be found. But do I have enough time to find it? There are less than twenty-four hours left before this ship is torn apart entering the Blackness. *Time is critical.*

This will be my last Captain's Log until the ball is found, or this ship destroyed. Until that moment I will be Dixon Hill, the best detective to ever walk the streets of the city by the bay. I just hope the best is good enough.

Section Two: Teamed Up

Benny the Banger's headquarters were in the back of a hardware store with a big front window and a door with the words HARDWARE AND TOOLS etched on the glass. Blinds had been drawn on both windows and Benny's goon didn't even slow down as he went past. Dix and Bev and the others followed the man around the corner and down the block to the alley where he stared down the dark, garbage-littered passageway between the buildings.

Dix motioned as they entered the alley for Whelan and the rest to spread out along the street and wait while he and the Luscious Bev went in with their shadow escorts.

"Oh, you'll want your guns back," Dix said, flipping the gun in his belt to the man who had done all the talking and was leading them. The other three goons got their weapons back as well.

"Thanks," the guy said, sticking the gun away inside his jacket.

The other three did the same.

"Don't mention it," Dix said.

"Don't worry 'bout that," the guy said, laughing.

The other three also nodded. It was clear that making a mistake with Benny and letting themselves get caught was a very bad thing.

The inside of the hardware store looked like the back room of any other store, with shelves of tools and boxes of nuts and bolts. A counter along the back wall was cluttered with hammers and saws.

"What is that smell?" Bev whispered.

"Cigar smoke," Dix said. The entire room was filled with thick cigar smoke. A cloud seemed to hang in the air and Dix's first impulse was to duck under it.

"Ughhh," Bev said, softly. "This is going to be toxic."

"This way," the guy said, opening up a side door that led into a well-lit and even smokier room. Five men sat around a green felt-covered table. Multicolored chips filled the center of the table and were stacked in front of each man. Cards were being shuffled by one man with his back to the door.

All the men were in their shirtsleeves, with their gun holsters showing. All five had guns.

And all five were smoking large cigars, and the ashtrays beside each man were full of old stogies. The smoke from each cigar seemed to drift upward and thicken the white cloud that filled the top half of the room. There was no window in the room to open.

"I see you brought me a guest," one man said. He stood, smoothed down his white silk shirt over his large stomach and motioned for Dix to come forward. He stood no more than five feet tall. Bev towered over him.

"I'm Benny," the short man said, smiling, the cigar a smoking stick in his left hand as he stepped around the table and extended his right hand for Dix to shake. "You play poker, Mr. Hill?"

Benny was dressed in the most expensive clothes of the bunch, and sweat had stained his shirt. He had the remains of his last meal dotting his shirt and the largest pile of chips in front of his position at the table. Clearly playing in this game was a losing proposition for anyone but Benny.

"No," Dix said. "I'm hear to make you an offer. A deal of sorts."

"A deal?" the man asked, smiling at Dix, then winking at Bev. "I heard you was looking for me. I'm just glad ta hear it wasn't to give me any problems."

"No problems," Dix said. "I'm looking for a small, gold-painted ball."

"About gumball size," Benny said, waving his hand for Dix to stop. "Yeah, I know, I heard. Why's this ball so important to you that you spent the entire night lookin' for it? I hear everywhere you look, people get killed."

Dix was stunned that the word had already reached

Benny. This little man was not someone to take lightly, that was for sure.

"Just say a special client of mine hired me to find it. It has no real value." Dix winked at Benny. "But he's paying me a big chunk of money to get it back for him. Something about it being his mother's."

"Well, Mr. Hill," Benny said, walking around in front of Bev and looking her over like she was something he wanted to purchase, "I sure wish I had that little ball."

"So do I," Dix said, "but I have a feeling Harvey Upstairs Benton has it."

Benny stopped his pacing like he had walked into a wall, turned, and looked hard into Dix's eyes. "And you want me to help you get it from Harvey?"

"Basically yes," Dix said.

"Why would I do dat? Sounds like more people gettin' killed to me." Benny shook his head and took a long pull on his cigar, letting the smoke out in a direct line at Dix. "I don't like when it happens to my men. Right, fellas?"

"Right," they all said, nodding and puffing.

"Because I have something you want," Dix said, "and that's why I want to deal."

Benny laughed, the sound high and almost shrill. The other men at the table laughed along with him, like trained seals, and all puffed on their cigars, adding even more thickness to the already thick, white air.

"What could you have, Mr. Hill, dat I would want?"

"I have two things, actually," Dix said. "The first I will give you to show you that my intentions are straight."

Dix nodded to Bev.

She reached under her coat, but by the time she could pull out the book, five guns were trained on her, and every man at the poker table had stood.

"Nothin' cute, now, doll-face," Benny said, the gun in his hand looking far too big for his frame. Yet Dix could tell there was no doubt the man knew how to use that big gun very well.

"Not a chance," Bev said. "Nothing cute, I promise."

She finished pulling out Slippery Stan Hand's ledger and handed it to Dix, who then handed it to Benny.

"You're givin' me a book?" The guy shook his head and laughed, putting his gun away in its holster. Again the rest of the men laughed, putting their guns away and sitting back down.

"What am I gonna do with a book?" Benny asked.

"Take a look at it," Dix said, nodding.

Benny flipped open the book, then suddenly got very interested. The pages flipped slower and slower, the sounds like a ticking clock in the silent room.

Then, with a glance at Dix, Benny went back to the start and flipped through the ledger again.

Dix just waited, letting the total effect of the book hook Benny into helping him.

"Where did ya get this?" Benny asked after the longest time, slapping the book closed.

"That, my friend," Dix said, "is my secret."

"This is Slippery Stan Hand's, right?"

"It is," Dix said. "And now it is yours, to do with as you see fit."

"To help you get into Harvey Upstairs Benton's place?"

"Yes," Dix said. "And when we do, and get to search it for the object I am looking for, I will then give you the other book."

"And what book is that?" Benny asked, clearly not making fun anymore.

"Cyrus Redblock had a ledger much like that one," Dix said, pointing at the book in Benny's hand, "only thicker. I would think that anyone who had those two ledgers would control this town, don't you?"

Benny stared at Dix for a long few seconds.

"You have Redblock's ledger?" Benny said, his voice almost a whisper.

"I do."

Benny stared at him a moment longer, then turned and headed across the room, where he pulled back an ugly picture of a half-naked woman exposing a wall safe. He spun the dial a few times, then opened the safe, put the ledger inside, spun the dial again, and slammed the picture back into position.

"Joe, Frank, gather up all the boys and meet in front of the store in twenty minutes."

The men at the poker table jumped up like the chairs

they were sitting on were spring-loaded. The cigars were stamped out in the ashtrays as they grabbed their coats.

The men were past Hill and Bev in a matter of seconds.

Benny walked across the room and looked up into Dix's eyes. "Mr. Hill, we have a deal. You just better not be double-crossing me."

Dix just smiled. "You get me and my people into Harvey Upstairs Benton's place and you have Red-block's ledger. That's our deal."

"Then we have work to do," Benny said, smiling. "Let's go."

Dix and Bev followed the little man out into the back room of the hardware store and into the alley. The cool, damp fresh air of the dark night felt wonderful. Bev coughed lightly, clearing out some of the smoke. Dix just enjoyed a few deep breaths before motioning for Mr. Whelan to round up the rest of the men and join them.

In ten minutes there were over thirty men, and one woman, standing in the empty street in front of the dark hardware store. Somehow, Dix had put together a small army to invade the last place the Heart of the Adjuster might be.

If they didn't find it in there, he didn't know what they were going to do in the last hours of their lives. But he did know he wasn't going to give up. Somewhere in this city was the Heart of the Adjuster.

Somewhere.

Clues from Dixon Hill's notebook in "The Case of the Missing Heart"

- Benny the Banger's goon says he hasn't seen any golden ball.
- Benny the Banger wants to rule the city and is just about to get his wish.
- Time is running low.

Chapter Eight

About Face

Section One: Showdown Escape

A CAT STREAKED ACROSS in front of them, ducking behind some garbage cans and then running down a dark alley, without interrupting their march. A stray dog dug in an overturned garbage can. They were the only things moving on the first four blocks of their dark walk toward Harvey Upstairs Benton's headquarters.

The rain was holding off, but the clouds and fog were swirling in low and fast, brushing past the tops of the buildings. It gave the night a black and white feel, with the wet pavement, dark stone and brick buildings, and the white clouds catching what little light there was from the occasional street lamp.

Benny had told Dix that Harvey's headquarters were in the back of a large car showroom. It was well guarded and there was no way to sneak up on it. "Goin' ta be hard to get into without a good, nasty fight."

"You willing to fight?" Dix had asked the gangster.

"For Redblock's book, I'm willin' to do just about anything," Benny had said, which had made Dix shudder at the thought of what he might have started.

Dix glanced around at his people following him. Bev was on his right, her heels clicking on the pavement. Maybe joining forces like this hadn't been such a good idea after all. He didn't want any of his people getting hurt. But at this point, with so little time left until everything was destroyed, Dix supposed he shouldn't care how much fight was needed.

They had to find that gold ball and get it back inside the Adjuster. And Harvey was the last logical person who might have it, or know who did have it, that Dix could think of.

And that fact worried Dix more than any other.

Suddenly in front of them, six cop cars sped into sight, coming from both directions, their engines like thunderclouds rumbling through the still night, echoing between the buildings full of sleeping people.

"We have company, boys," Benny said.

Dix couldn't believe this was happening. They couldn't be stopped now, not so close to this last chance.

He motioned for his people to stop and stay back.

Benny didn't seem to notice that Dix had fallen back as he and his men all drew their guns and kept on going, slowly spreading out over the entire street and sidewalk.

"Not looking good for this plan," Bev whispered.

Dix could do nothing but agree. It didn't look good at all. The last thing he wanted was police involvement.

"How had they known and gotten such a force in front of us so quickly?" Bev asked, her voice just above a whisper.

"Clearly Benny's organization has a very large leak in it," Dix said.

"About the size of a drain pipe I would say," Bev said.

The cop cars slid to a stop, blocking the road, their flashing lights covering the buildings and the fast moving clouds and fog overhead with blood-red warnings.

The entire world had turned red it seemed. Dix didn't like the look of that at all.

He glanced around and then motioned for his people to move toward the sidewalk on the right as more cop cars roared in behind them, blocking the intersection they had just come through as well.

"Nice move," Dix said about their retreat being cut off, more to himself than anyone.

The army he had formed to take down Harvey Upstairs Benton was now surrounded by police and split into two groups. One marching into sure death, the other retreating, trying to figure a way out.

Dix knew that they were going to be lucky to get out of this alive, let alone without being arrested and detained.

And they didn't have time to be arrested. That was also sure death.

"Get out of our way," Benny the Banger shouted to the police in front of him who had gotten out of their cars and were using them as cover, guns drawn. "We're just out for a peaceful walk. No need to be bothering us."

"Then you won't mind stoppin' and talkin', will ya?" a cop's voice answered back.

"Our fight's not with you," Benny said, his voice echoing like a bell of doom through the street, bouncing off the red-tinted buildings.

"But a fight with us is what you're going to get," the cop said, "unless you stop. Now!"

Benny and his men clearly were not going to stop.

"Yeah, Dix," Bell shouted from a car a half block behind where Dix had his people. "No fight tonight?"

"Follow me," Dix said to his people, just loud enough for them to hear. "And no guns. Get your hands in the air."

Everyone nodded and followed his lead as Dix put his hands up and moved toward where he could see Detective Bell standing in front of one of the cars.

"You're right, of course," Dix said, just loud enough for Bell and the other cops to hear.

He glanced over his shoulder. Benny and the twenty men who were following him were still walking right at the cop cars, spreading out more and more as they went. It looked like a gunfight in an old western between two rival outlaw gangs.

From what Dix could tell, Benny hadn't even noticed that Dix and his people were missing.

"Stop now!" a cop ordered, his voice carrying all the way down the street. "Don't be stupid, Benny."

Benny kept on being very stupid, as far as Dix was concerned.

"Why is he doing that?" Bev asked.

"I have no idea," Dix said, "but we need to get out of the cross fire and fast."

"This entire town has gone crazy tonight," Whelan said.

"You'll get no argument from me on that," Dix said.

Dix reached the corner building and turned, walked ten steps and stopped, making sure the rest of his people got around that corner as well. Safe, at least from the direct line of fire.

They were just in time.

Someone fired first, a single lone gunshot like the shot at the start of a race. The next instant there was so much gunfire going on it sounded like one continuous blast of sound, echoing and bouncing off the buildings.

Lights flashed on in every room as glass smashed and bullets thudded into the sides of the cop cars.

Display windows in a clothing store smashed inward, ripping apart a woman's dress in the window.

Lieutenant Bell, who had started toward Dix, suddenly dove for cover behind a car, then came up on the hood and started to return fire at Benny and his men.

"Let's get out of here," Bev said as a bullet bounced

off a nearby building and smashed into a window over their heads, sending glass showering down on them.

Dix could not have agreed more. "Keep your hands in the air, like you are surrendering," Dix ordered his people over the roar of gunfire. "Follow me, slowly."

The fight went on, bullets pounding into police cars with the sound of a child hitting dull drums.

Glass smashed, one man screamed in pain.

Dix could see that Detective Bell was more than busy and very pinned down behind his car, both by the fire from Benny's men and the stray shots from the other cops down the road. There was no chance he could pay them the slightest bit of attention. And since they had stopped and surrendered, there was no point that he should.

Dix eased them all away from the fight, step by step along the dark side street.

Slowly the gunfire started to decrease. It was clear that Benny and his men had stood no chance in the middle of that road. And why Benny had even tried was beyond Dix. This world was just making no sense at all anymore.

"Okay, hands down," Dix said as they reached the middle of the block. "Let's go. Follow me."

With that he picked up speed, expecting to hear shouts to stop behind them at any moment, but the fight was still going on.

Another man screamed in pain, and more bullets bounced off stone.

The front window of one of the cop cars exploded.

But the sound of the gunfire was now like a thunderstorm echoing in the distance, sometimes a full second of quiet between shots.

Clearly some of Benny's men had found cover along the middle of the block and were holding off the cops from both sides far longer than Dix would have thought possible. But he didn't want to see the blood running in that street right now. The gutters would have to be full of it.

Dix, with Bev right beside him, reached the corner, crossed the street, and turned away from the fight, going in the opposite direction from the one they had been headed in the first time.

The last of the gunfire still echoed behind them, but it was amazing how turning one corner could dim it, make it less intrusive and pounding.

At the next corner Dix turned again, the sounds of his, Bev's, and the others' footsteps now louder than the last few shots of the fight.

Finally the shooting stopped.

Dix halted right in the middle of the block, right in front of an alley opening.

The silence of the city clamped down on them like a vise. All of them were breathing hard.

"Everyone all right?" Dix asked.

"Shaken," Bev said.

The rest nodded they were fine as they brushed glass out of their hair or off their coats and hats.

"Okay," Dix said, "they're going to wonder what happened to us right about now."

Dix studied the faces of his people. Bev looked flushed, even in the dark street light, Whelan had lost his hat somewhere, and Carter's face was pale and he was breathing hard. The others were staring at him, taking deep breaths of the cold night air, their breath white clouds in front of their faces.

"We're running out of time," Bev said.

Dix knew that as well as anyone. "I want everyone to spread out and work their way back to my office. If you are stopped by the police, say nothing about where you are headed."

Everyone nodded.

"Bev, you and I are going to go see if we can just talk to Harvey Upstairs Benton. Who knows, maybe he's willing to cut a deal."

"At this point anything is worth a try," Bev said.

Dix couldn't agree more.

"If we don't return in half an hour everyone report to Mr. Riker."

Again everyone nodded.

"Let's go, people," Dix said.

With that, they turned and started off, a few heading back toward the intersection they had just come through, others starting across the street toward the next intersection, their footsteps the only sound on the silent, dark street.

Dix and Bev stayed on the sidewalk, walking as fast as Bev's high heels would allow them to go.

And with each step more time passed, time they couldn't afford to lose or waste.

Section Two: Dealing with the Devil

Dix hovered over Bev, his back to the street, his coat spread out for cover as the two of them crouched inside a deep doorway, hiding as a cop car passed, slowly, looking for them.

The sound of the car's engine was loud in the street, echoing off the dark windows and empty pavement. Dix held his breath until the car turned the corner and the sound faded, then he exhaled and stood. It had been very lucky for them that they had heard it coming.

He reached down and helped Bev up. "You all right?"

She nodded, brushing off her skirt and straightening her hair and coat.

Dix eased carefully to the edge of the arched doorway and looked out at the street.

Deserted.

"Too close," Bev said as they stepped out of the doorway and started again toward Harvey Upstairs Benton's headquarters.

"With a little more than a few hours left, I think everything is too close," Dix said.

His stomach was tied in a knot, and he didn't know if that was from worry or from not eating for so long. He pushed the discomfort away and focused on what he had to do coming up.

And if he had missed anything.

Bev said nothing, her heels clicking on the sidewalk, sharp offbeats to his footsteps.

Dix had a strong feeling they weren't going to find

the Heart of the Adjuster at Harvey's place. Yet it was the only logical thing he could think of to try at the moment, so they had to do it. Nothing after this made any sense at all.

Suddenly, as if someone had tossed a switch, the weather shifted. On one block it had seemed like a normal night, with the fog swirling over them, threatening rain at any moment; on the next block it got bitingly cold and snow drifted down in between the buildings.

"Snow in the city by the bay," Bev said, holding out her hand and catching a few flakes as they walked. "Now that is something you don't see very often."

"Along the lines of people coming back to life," Dix said.

"Yeah, along those lines."

In front of them Dix could see the corner of Harvey's car dealership. "Hands up."

Bev did as he said without missing a stride or dropping her purse.

Holding their hands in the air, they stepped out into the intersection and headed for the front door of Harvey Upstairs Benton's headquarters.

A very large man, with a smashed-in nose and a gun impossibly large, stepped toward them. Snow, like a bad case of dandruff, covered his shoulders and hair.

"We came to see your boss," Dix said. "We have an offer he's going to want to hear."

"He knows you was comin'," the guy said.

Dix glanced at Bev, then shrugged. At this point nothing was surprising him.

With the big gun the guy with the damaged nose waved them toward the front door of the car dealership. Inside the heat was on and the snow melted off them almost instantly. Two other men came forward, also pointing guns at them.

"Armed?" one of them asked.

"Of course," Dix said, opening up his coat and showing them the gun.

"That's where it stays," one man said.

"I understand," Dix said. "I'm here to deal, not fight."

"Smart move," the guy said. "Healthy."

He pointed the way toward a door in the back, leaving the big guy with the smashed nose to move back out into the snow to stand guard.

Dix and Bev went through the door and down a long hall to an office filled with pictures of cars, a large desk, and not much else. A man in an expensive pinstriped suit sat behind the desk doing paperwork. He glanced up as they entered and the two goons took up positions on both sides of the door behind them.

Harvey Upstairs Benton looked just like a car dealer. The minute he looked up at them he flashed a smile that was about as phony and put-on as smiles came. His hair was slicked back and thinning, and he wore too many rings.

"Mr. Hill," Harvey said, "I hear you are looking for me."

"Actually," Dix said, "I'm looking for a small ball,

about so big." Dix showed him the size, then went on. "Painted gold."

"And this ball is worth waltzing in here in the middle of the night to ask me about?"

"It is," Dix said.

"Must be a valuable ball," Harvey said.

"To a few people, it is," Dix said. "To everyone else, it is worthless."

"And if I had this ball," Harvey said, "you'd be willing to pay for it? Am I right?"

Dix could feel his stomach twist. Was it possible this man actually had the Heart of the Adjuster? "I would."

Harvey laughed. "And just what might you have that I could use?"

"First," Dix said, staring into Harvey's cold eyes, "to show my good faith, I'll give you some information you can use right now."

Harvey stopped smiling and leaned back in his chair. "I'm waiting."

"In the wall safe behind an ugly picture, in the back room of Benny the Banger's hardware store, is Slippery Stan Hand's ledger book. And I would imagine Benny's as well."

"You mean the book that records all Stan's deals?" Harvey asked, clearly testing Dix.

"That's the one, with names and times and amounts and everything."

"So what makes you think I can get in there now?" Harvey asked.

Dix looked at him with surprise. He had known that

Dix and Bev were coming to talk to him, but he hadn't known about the gunfight just six blocks away. That didn't make sense, but he couldn't tell if Harvey was playing him along or not.

"The cops are cleaning up what is left of Benny and his gang in the middle of the street about six blocks from here," Dix said. "He was headed this way to take you on, but the police got there first."

Harvey smiled, and then laughed, deep and low, and very, very mean. But neither the laugh, nor the smile, got to his eyes. "I know," Harvey said. "I was the one that tipped the cops off to Benny's and your plan."

Dix knew they were in trouble. This guy was a long ways in front of them on many fronts.

Harvey reached into the drawer and pulled out a ledger book and flipped it onto the desk. "I assume you are talking about this book," Harvey said. "I had my boys pick it up before you and your mob was two blocks from Benny's place."

Dix said nothing. Clearly this man knew far, far more than he was letting on. And until Dix knew exactly what this man wanted and what he didn't, anything Dix might say could get him and Bev killed.

"So Mr. Hill, what is it you can offer me?"

"I would assume you know," Dix said, staring into the depths of those dark, evil eyes.

Again Harvey laughed, like a salesman laughing at a joke from a customer, even though he'd heard it a thousand times. "Very good, Mr. Hill. I know why you have such a reputation."

Dix said nothing.

"How about Redblock's ledger?" Harvey asked. "Are you willing to give me Redblock's ledger, assuming you have it, for this gold ball of yours?"

"I am," Dix said. He had no doubt that Harvey knew he had it.

Harvey again leaned back. "Too bad I don't have your little ball. If I did, I honestly would give it to you. But I don't, I'm afraid to say."

Dix kept quiet. He had guessed and felt, deep in his gut, almost from the moment they had started talking, that Harvey didn't have the ball and had just been playing them. Now it was a matter of getting out of here alive and trying to look somewhere else in what little time they had left.

"So," Harvey said, smiling at Dix and then winking at Bev, "how about I trade you your lives for Redblock's book instead? That sound like a fair trade?"

"I assume you keep your deals and are an honorable man," Dix said.

Harvey laughed. "Of course I'm not honorable. I sell used cars. But you have to know that I have some honor, since you're still standing there, alive."

Dix kept his mouth shut and Harvey went on.

"In this case, I will give you my word that you can leave alive and well if I have Redblock's ledger. And when I say you can trust my word, you can trust it."

"Besides," Dix said, "if you have the ledger, you have no reason to bother killing us."

"Well," Harvey said, "you do have a good point

there. Who knows when I might need a detective on my side down the road, especially someone as good as you are."

Dix nodded, reached into his coat.

Guns cocked behind them and Dix froze. Harvey put up his hand for his men to hold it. "Can't you see that Mr. Hill here is an honorable man who wouldn't want this beautiful woman friend of his hurt."

Dix didn't bother to look around at the guns pointed at him. Instead he pulled out the ledger from the back of his belt, then flipped it onto the desk in front of Harvey Upstairs Benton. It landed with a thud that felt very, very final.

Harvey quickly glanced through it, then nodded and closed the book. "Escort Mr. Hill and his lovely date out. And Mr. Hill, if you ever need a car, I'll give you a deal."

"Thanks," Dix said.

Harvey tapped the ledger and smiled. "For bringing me this, I owe you that much."

"Just let me know if you find that ball in the next few hours," Dix said. "After that it's not going to matter."

Harvey frowned as Dix turned and, with one hand on Bev's elbow, went out the door, down the hallway, and back out into the gently falling snow as the two goons with guns followed them.

They turned and at a fast walk headed for Dix's office.

If the situation wasn't so desperate, the snow might actually have been beautiful to walk in. It didn't snow that often in the city by the bay.

Section Three: Once More Into the Breach

About two blocks from Harvey's car dealership, it stopped snowing; a block later it started raining; a block after that the clouds cleared and the stars came out. Dix felt almost beat up, not only by the weather, but by the night that would never end. He was cold, damp, and angry at himself.

Dixon Hill and the Luscious Bev walked through the smorgasbord of weather, saying nothing. Dix didn't even much notice the changes. Pretty soon, in a few short hours, the city would be gone, and everything else as well, and all because he couldn't find a small golden ball.

After eight long blocks of silence, eight long blocks of Dix going over and over every detail he could think of, they reached his office building. He was so lost in thought, he almost walked past it. Bev had to tug on his arm to get him to stop and turn in.

"Any luck, boss?" Mr. Whelan asked from his position to the right of the stairs outside.

"Not yet, I'm afraid," Dix said. "You have guards set up?"

"Both directions down the sidewalk," Whelan said.

"Good." Dix wasn't sure why he was still having them stay on guard, but better to be warned about something coming at them than not.

Dix and Bev climbed the outside steps and went inside, then climbed up to the second floor. The smell of Jessica Daniels' perfume still lingered faintly in the background. Her blood on the carpet was gone in the upper hallway. In both directions the hall seemed empty, almost forecasting how everything was going to be shortly.

"Who do you think shot Jessica?" Bev asked as they got to the top.

Dix pointed to the lack of blood spot in the carpet. "I suppose we could always go ask her. But my guess would be one of Harvey's goons trying to get Stan Hand's ledger."

Bev nodded. "So would mine."

Three of Dix's men sat in the outer office. Carter, Daniels, and Williams. "Find it?" Carter asked as all three men stood.

"No," Dix said as Mr. Data opened the door from the inner office. He no longer smelled of death and rotting flesh, but was dressed in what looked like the same suit.

"So where do we look next, boss?" Mr. Data asked.

"You know," Dix said, moving inside and hanging up his hat and coat, "I honestly don't have a clue."

He moved around and dropped into his chair as the others took up positions around the room.

Silence filled the office.

The silence of death and despair.

Dix could feel it, wanted to fight it. Yet he had nothing to hold up to stop it.

"Well," Bev said, "we're not going to find it sitting around here. Why not go over what happened again?"

"Exactly," Mr. Data said. "Go back to the crime

scene to find that one clue we missed the first time. It happens a lot in detective novels."

"Mr. Data," Dix said, "this isn't a novel. And the crime scene was just out there in the hallway, remember?"

"Vividly," Mr. Data said.

"What can it hurt?" Bev said, moving over and pulling Dix up out of his chair. "Let's run through what happened one more time, just to make sure we haven't missed anything before we give up on this and try something else."

Dix let himself be pushed. She was right. Moving, acting was their only hope at this point, even though acting might solve little. At least he was doing something.

All six of them moved out into the hallway.

"This was where the Adjuster ended up," Mr. Data said. He pointed to an exact spot in the middle of the hall, right at the top of the stairway.

"And where were you, Mr. Data?" Bev asked.

"We were working to open the door here," Mr. Data said, taking ten steps down the hall toward the wall where Dix knew the door was. It was out of sight of both where the Adjuster sat and the staircase.

Bev looked at where the door in the wall was, then back at the spot where the Adjuster had sat.

"What are you thinking?" Dix asked.

Bev motioned for him to wait, then moved down the stairs, her heels clicking on the hard stairs as everyone stood in silence and watched. She stopped on the landing and looked back up at them. "How high was the Adjuster?" she asked.

Mr. Data held his hand about knee high.

The Luscious Bev started back up the staircase.

"How high was the Heart of the Adjuster?" she asked.

Date knelt and put his right hand into a fist and put it below his left. It was a pretty good approximation of how the golden ball had sat in the small machine.

Bev immediately stopped and then backed up almost to the landing. "So anyone my height, at this point, would see the Heart of the Adjuster as they were coming up the stairs."

"Exactly," Dix said.

"Were you and La Forge talking while you worked?" Bev asked.

"Yes," Mr. Data said. "We were discussing ways of getting the door open."

"So anyone coming up the stairs would have heard you, just about the time they saw the golden ball?"

"It would have been possible, yes," Mr. Data said.

"Which was why it was so easy to take," Dix said.

Bev nodded. "I understand that." She looked around the staircase, then up at Dix. "But my question is, why would anyone be coming up these stairs?"

"To see me," Dix said. "There's no office in this building but mine."

Suddenly his words, hanging in the air, caught him like a hammer. "Of course. We've been thinking that some regular thief took it and then would sell the

Heart, therefore allowing the Heart to make its way up to one of the crime bosses in the city."

"Logical thinking," Mr. Data said, "because that is how all crime works in this city. It is controlled by the bosses, so anything stolen, they would know about."

Dix nodded. It was the reason they had gone after the crime bosses so hard. If something was stolen in this city, one of the bosses had it, or knew where it was. Usually that someone was Cyrus Redblock, but that wasn't the case at the moment.

"But why would a regular thief be in this old building?"

"Good question, boss," Mr. Data said.

Bev smiled at Dix, knowing he had jumped ahead of her. "What happened if whoever took it wasn't normally a thief?" she asked. "And then, if not a regular city thief, wouldn't know how to sell it to one of the bosses."

"Exactly," Dix said. He spun and headed back into his office. Why hadn't he thought of this hours ago? He had been so wrapped up in walking on one road, he hadn't noticed that there might be other roads as well.

"Where are you going, boss?" Mr. Data asked as he and the others followed Dix back inside.

"To see if I had an appointment about the time you were trying to fix that door," Dix said over his shoulder. "I want to find out who had a reason to come up those stairs."

Dix opened the top drawer of the desk in the outer office, pulled out his appointment book, and flipped it open. "Mr. Data, what time of the day would you estimate it was when the Heart was stolen?"

"About five in the evening in this city's time," Mr. Data said, "give or take fifteen minutes. I do not believe I can be any more accurate than that, boss, considering the circumstances of the reality of this world."

"Close enough," Dix said.

He flipped to the right page and scanned down the mostly empty appointment book. There were only two names anywhere near that five P.M. time. The first was Arnie Andrews, the husband of actress Marci Andrews.

Marci, one of Dix's favorite actresses in the city, had been killed at her stage door, and he had been working on his own to solve her case, talking to both her husband and her ex-lover, Brad Barringer. It seemed he had had an appointment with Arnie Andrews at 4:45 that day.

Dix, of course, had not made it to the appointment, due to other outside problems, but had Arnie made it? That was a critical question.

The other name on the list was a one-word name, circled, with the words "Dinner with wife" scrawled out beside the name.

Bell.

Five P.M. appointment.

Detective Bell, his friend.

Dix just stared at the name, not really believing it was possible.

Yet there it was.

Detective Bell had been scheduled to come up those

stairs right at five, right at the time the Heart of the Adjuster had been stolen.

If Bell had taken it, what did they now need to do to get it back?

Dix stared at the names for a few long seconds, then made his decision.

"Mr. Data," Dix said, looking up at the five others in the office. "How much time do we have? Approximately."

"One hour and forty-five minutes," Mr. Data said.

Those words slammed down the fear and worry like a heavy weight, pressing on all of them.

Two suspects and only one hour and forty-five minutes to find a golden ball. They had no choice. They had to go after both at the same time.

"Mr. Data, you and Mr. Carter and two of the others downstairs go and find Arnie Andrews and search his apartment. If you don't find the Heart, bring him back here. I don't care how you do it. Just don't kill him. We need to talk to him."

He scribbled Arnie Andrews' address on a piece of paper and handed it to Mr. Data. "Don't waste any time."

"Understood," Mr. Data said, snapping around and heading for the door with Mr. Carter right behind him.

"And what are we going to do?" Bev asked. Her face was white, the worry deep in her eyes.

Dix scooted the appointment book over and moved it so Bev and the other two could read it.

"Oh, my," Bev said under her breath.

"We're going to set up a trap for a cop," Dix said. He

smiled at the Luscious Bev. "And you're going to be the bait."

Clues from Dixon Hill's notebook in "The Case of the Missing Heart"

- Benny the Banger is either dead, recovering from being dead, or in jail.
- Harvey Upstairs Benton did not have the ball, but managed to get both ledgers anyway.
- Either Arnie Andrews or Detective Bell had the opportunity to take the Heart of the Adjuster.

Chapter Nine

Old Cases, Old Friends

Section One: Confrontation

OUTSIDE DIX'S OFFICE WINDOWS, the perpetual night of the city by the bay continued. The hard rain again pounded the street and rattled the windows. It was coming down so heavy that it was impossible to see more than twenty paces between the buildings.

The gutters were filling up as the rain came down faster than the drainage could take it away. Every so often a burst of wind would swirl the rain, sending it sideways across the window instead of down to the street.

Inside, the night's chill had backed off some as the old radiator cracked to life and worked to fight the dampness. Dix sat alone, thinking, letting the last minutes of this city tick past slowly, grinding their way toward the end of everything he knew and cared about.

A few minutes earlier Bev had made the phone call to Detective Bell like a pro, sitting on the edge of his desk, her legs crossed, her smile firmly in place. Her voice had had just enough panic in it to make it believable, yet calm enough to make herself understood. Dix was convinced she could have been a great actress if she had wanted to go that way.

While she had talked, Dix had sat behind his desk and smiled back at her, listening to her every word, nodding at how perfectly she worked the bait.

"Detective Bell, this is Bev, the friend of Dixon Hill's." Her voice had been hurried and insistent, just as it would have been if Dix had really been hurt.

She listened for a very short moment as Bell said something Dix couldn't hear.

"No, you don't understand," Bev had said, making her voice sound as if it might break. "Dix was hit when we were trying to get away earlier. I don't think he's going to make it."

There had been another pause on Bev's end as Bell reacted. She had winked at Dix, then focused back on the call.

"We carried him back here. He wants to talk to you. He's been asking for you when he is awake. I thought I'd better call you at once. There isn't much time left."

There had been another short pause as she listened.

"We're in his office. Please hurry."

Pause again.

Dix had watched as she nodded to something Bell was telling her.

"Thank you, Detective Bell."

She had reached across and dropped the phone in its cradle like it was some sort of garbage that she didn't really want to touch and was tossing away.

"He's on his way. Five minutes tops he said."

"You're good at that," Dix had said as he stood and moved around the desk.

"I'm a woman," the Luscious Bev had said, smiling at him and batting her eyes.

That look had stopped him cold. "You mean because you are a woman, you can naturally fool men and lie to them?"

"What do you think?" she had asked, smiling at him in the way that told him he was being played like a fine violin. Sometimes he enjoyed it, at that moment he hadn't been so sure.

"I'm going down to make sure everyone knows what they are supposed to do."

"Not a good idea," Bev had said, hopping off the corner of the desk. "I'll do it, you stay here. We can't have Bell see you walking around when you are supposed to be dying, now can we?"

Dix had agreed with her. She had been right.

"Stay put," she had said and headed out the door.

When the door closed he had moved behind his desk and taken out his gun, making sure it was loaded and ready to use. Then he had put it on the desktop and sat down. For the first time since the Heart of the Adjuster had been taken, he had a moment alone to think.

And now that was what he was doing.

Thinking, feeling the time tick away like blood draining from a wounded man.

As Mr. Data and Bev had suggested earlier, once he got a moment to review everything, he started back at the beginning, working through how this had gotten started, running over the different things that had happened, checking details, looking for any clue as to who might have taken the Heart.

Anything he might have missed.

He didn't see anything.

He had taken a great deal of precious time going through the crime bosses, making sure that a common thief on the street hadn't taken the Heart and sold it to them. It had been a logical assumption, especially considering what had happened to Redblock and the nature of crime in this city.

But now that the bosses were eliminated, he reviewed the two remaining suspects.

Arnie Andrews, the husband of murdered actress Marci Andrews, had had a reason to be climbing those stairs at about the time the Adjuster was sitting unguarded. But was he the type to see the gold ball and instantly want to take it? That was going to be a question he had to find an answer to quickly.

Then there was Detective Bell. Bell had bent laws and done favors in most of the ten cases Dix had worked, so Dix knew he was no innocent. But Bell was also a friend. Dix had had a standing invite to go home with Bell and meet his wife and kids and have dinner. Would Bell take something from a friend?

And most important, Bell knew that Dix was looking for the Heart. He might not know how important it was, but he knew Dix thought it important. And if he had taken it, he might have found a way to give it back by now.

But he might not have, either.

Dix was going to have to tread lightly when talking to his old friend. If Bell hadn't taken the Heart, then that just left Arnie Andrews. And with Mr. Data searching Andrews' apartment, that lead was being run down at the same time.

There were clicking footsteps on the stairs and in the hallway and a moment later Bev came back in, brushing the rain off her coat. "Everyone is in place and will come up behind Detective Bell. Once he's in the building, he won't be getting out."

She moved over to the window and glanced out through the rain. "He just pulled up."

"Okay," Dix said, "stand off to one side. This is between me and Bell."

Bev nodded, closed the door, and then moved over to a spot near the window where she leaned against the wall, her arms crossed. Dix remained seated behind his desk, pretending he had been doing just standard paperwork.

The heavy footsteps echoed through the building as Bell ran up the stairs and through the outer office. He opened the inner office door and then froze, rain dripping from his coat and hat.

"Thanks for coming," Dix said. "Come on in and close the door. Have a seat."

"What is this?" Bell demanded, staring at Dix sitting obviously unhurt behind his desk. "People coming back from the dead before they die now?"

"I need to ask you some blunt questions, and I didn't have time to go find you," Dix said.

"Yeah, so," Bell said, "you knew where I was."

Dix shook his head. "No, I needed you here. And it had to be fast. We are all almost out of time."

"So you told her to lie to me?" Bell asked, clearly angry, motioning at Bev. "What kind of friend would do that to another friend?"

"The same kind of friend that would ask you if you took the Heart of the Adjuster I've been looking for."

Now Bell looked really stunned.

"Sit for a minute," Dix said, before Bell could say anything more, "and let me explain why I would even ask that question. And why I had to lie to get you here."

Bell stared at Dix, then with a glance at Bev, pushed the door closed and sat in the chair facing Dix's desk. He brushed water off his coat and then took his hat off and shook it at the floor.

"Take a look at this," Dix said, sliding his appointment book toward the detective, flipping it over so Bell could read it. "The Adjuster with the gold-looking Heart was sitting at the top of the stairs out in the hall, unguarded for about five minutes, somewhere between 4:45 and 5:15. That was when it was taken."

Bell studied the appointment book, then nodded and slid it back at Bell.

"I know you're a basically honest man," Dix said.

"Your name does not appear anywhere in either Red-block's ledger or Slippery Stan Hand's records."

"That's good to hear," Bell said, clearly still angry, "since I wouldn't take a thin dime from either of those two slimeballs." He flipped his still wet hat onto Dix's desk.

Dix ignored Bell and his actions and anger and went on.

"I don't know how to tell you how important that little ball is to the continued existence of this entire city. You're just going to have to believe me that if we don't find it in the next ninety minutes, we will all die. You, me, your wife. Everyone."

"Ninety minutes?" Bell said, waving away Dix's statement like it was a bug flying in front of his face. "Ah, come on, quit pullin' my leg. This is getting old."

"I am not kidding," Dix said, staring at his friend. "I wish I were."

Bell stared right back at Dix. Then after a moment Bell said, "You're not kidding, are you?"

"No."

"You said this had something to do with the strange weather and this night that will never end?"

"It does," Dix said.

"And with me and the others coming back alive?"

Dix nodded.

Bell took a deep breath and sat back. "All right, I can see why you had to ask when you saw this appointment book. You had to talk to everyone who might have come up the stairs at the point the thing was taken, right?"

Dix nodded.

"Makes sense, friendship or no friendship. I'd have done the same thing."

"Exactly," Dix said.

"Still a cheap trick, telling me you were hurt."

"It got you here," Dix said, smiling. He was glad that he had managed to get through Bell's anger to the smart detective mind in there. He was going to need Bell's help.

"Okay, I'll tell you this," Bell said. "I didn't take the gold ball. In fact, this entire day and long night have been so crazy, I forgot you were goin' to have dinner with us. I haven't been home, or had a good meal in so long, I have almost forgotten what my wife looks like."

He paused and thought for a moment. Dix didn't interrupt. Bev also stayed silent, hands crossed over her chest, just watching and waiting.

Finally Bell said, "I honestly have no idea where I was right at the time I was supposed to be here, since time and this night have gone totally bonkers. More than likely I was trying to keep somebody from shooting somebody else, or doing paperwork on somebody."

He looked directly into Dix's eyes and kept talking. "So I didn't come up those stairs to even see the thing you're looking for. To be honest with you, I wish I had. I might have stopped whoever took it, and we'd be eating dinner with my wife and smoking cigars on the steps."

Dix stared at his friend for the longest time, then

nodded. "Good enough for me. Sorry to have to trick you to get you over here."

"Had me scared to death," Bell said, laughing. "So who's the other name on that list? It rings a bell, but I'm so tired I can't place it right off."

"Husband of Marci Andrews, the murdered actress."

Bell snapped his fingers. "That's right. You were working that case. Seems like a long time ago now."

"That it does," Dix admitted.

"So I can tell you," Bell said, "that you are going to need my help shaking him down."

"I don't think so," Dix said. "I have Mr. Data and a few others searching his apartment. If they don't find the Heart, they're going to bring Andrews here."

Bell laughed and took his hat from Dix's desk. "That's going to be some trick."

Dix looked at Bell. "Why?"

"The cops working the Marci Andrews murder arrested Arnie Andrews about ten minutes before I got shot in that doorway." Bell said. "He's sitting in a holding cell downtown right now. Been there all night."

Section Two: Sweat Drips Just Like Blood

Dix had Bev wait in his office with instructions to call him at once when Mr. Data returned, then headed out into the heavy rain with Detective Bell. The water pounded at him, closing in the already closed-in world around him, making him feel as if he were fighting against everything, simply trying to get to the car.

Even though Dix had sworn he would never ride with Bell again, this time Bell's speed didn't bother him. They needed all the speed they could find as each second ticked them closer to the end.

Four minutes later they were brushing the water off their coats and hats and heading into the interrogation room at police headquarters.

Bell had used Dix's phone to call ahead and have Arnie Andrews put in the interrogation room. Dix had sat in that room, in that hot seat, on his first case, the one he called "The Big Good-bye." It hadn't been fun after a short time.

If he and Bell had anything to do with it, the seat wasn't going to be fun for Arnie Andrews either. They were going to have to work fast. They didn't have the time to slowly sweat anything out of this guy.

Bell went in first and nodded for the guard to leave. Dix closed the door behind him.

Arnie Andrews was seated under the hot light, his hands cuffed behind his back. His hair was short and cut to fashion, his clothes looked expensive, and he was already starting to sweat.

Dix studied him, trying to look for any weakness. Andrews had the chin of an actor and the blue eyes to go along with the chin. Dix had talked to him once before, when he first had started on the case of Marci Andrews' murder. He had thought Arnie was a slimeball then, and seeing him sitting under the hot light, hands cuffed, didn't change that opinion in the slightest.

Bell had said on the way downtown that if he remembered right, they had found the gun that had killed Marci in Andrews' car, tucked under the back seat. Had her blood on it. That had been enough to get him arrested.

"So, Andrews," Bell said, taking off his coat and then his jacket and slinging them over the back of a nearby chair. "Comfortable?"

"No," Andrews said, pulling against the handcuffs.

Dix took off his coat and jacket as well and laid them on another chair, then loosened his tie.

"You're going to have to be more talkative than that," Bell said, walking around Andrews like a cat stalking a wounded and trapped bird, "if you want to get out of here anytime soon."

"I told the other cops earlier, I didn't kill Marci," Andrews said.

Bell laughed. "And I suppose you don't know how the gun got in your car either?"

"I don't, I swear," Andrews said, twisting to follow Bell as he moved around and around him. "I don't own a gun, don't even like guns, even when they're props on stage. You can ask anyone. Honest."

Bell nodded, patting Andrews on the cheek just a little too hard. "Now talking was easy, wasn't it? Big long sentences. I like that, and you keep me happy, you'll get out of here faster."

Andrews nodded real quick, his head bobbing like a lovesick puppy wanting to please a master. Dix almost expected his tongue to hang out as well.

"Okay, look," Dix said, moving up and smiling at

Andrews. "How about we start with some easy stuff, then work backward. That work for you?"

"Start anywhere you want," Andrews said. "I don't care. I still didn't kill my wife. I loved her."

"Sure you did," Dix said.

"Well," Bell said, "you convince us of that and we'll drive you home. All right with you?"

Andrews nodded.

"Start with the last twenty-four hours," Dix said. "What did you do yesterday after you got out of bed?"

"Breakfast at the deli, then I went down to the theater," Andrews said. "Just like I do every morning. I'm working on the new play that starts there in two weeks."

"So how long did you stay at the theater?" Bell asked. "And can people vouch for you?"

"Sure," Andrews said. "I was onstage most of the time, rehearsing. I stayed until about four-thirty, then headed to your office, Hill."

He almost spat Dix's name.

"What did you see there?" Dix asked, his stomach twisting at how long this was taking. Every minute seemed to stretch, yet flash past. There just weren't that many minutes left.

"Not you," Andrews said, "that's for sure. I got there about twenty-till-five, waited around a few minutes and then got disgusted that you'd stood me up, so I left. I don't know why you wanted to talk to me in the first place."

"No one was there?" Dix asked. "This is important

to convince us you are telling the truth. Was there anything strange-looking in the hallway?"

"Nothing but some stray cat," Andrews said. "Why?"

"So what did you do next?" Bell asked as Dix turned away to hide his disappointment. He believed Andrews. The guy hadn't been lying at all.

"I went from there down to the Banner Restaurant," Andrews said. "You can ask the barkeep there. It's a good ten-minute walk, maybe longer, and he served me my first drink right before five. Then I had dinner. You want to know what I ate? Or drank? I can tell you. I was on my way home when the cops got me. And I haven't had anything to eat since."

Dix felt his stomach sinking, the hope draining away. If Andrews was telling the truth, and he really had no reason to lie, then he hadn't been there when the Adjuster was there.

"Don't worry," Bell said, again slapping Andrews' face a little too hard, "you'll be fed as soon as the sun comes up."

At that moment the door to the interrogation room opened and a man stuck his head in the door. "Hill, you got a call."

Dix nodded to Bell and followed the man out and down the hallway where he pointed to a phone lying beside its cradle on a counter.

He grabbed the phone like it was a lifeline. "Dixon Hill here."

"This is Bev. Mr. Data didn't find anything at Arnie Andrews' apartment."

Dix wasn't surprised, after what Arnie had just told them. "Did Mr. Data search it carefully?"

"Very carefully," Bev said. "But Mr. Data tells me he thinks the cops had already searched it. If Andrews took the Heart, it might be locked up there at the station somewhere in some sort of evidence room."

"Good point," Dix said. "I'll have Bell check it out."

"Also, a Brad Barringer called a few minutes ago," Bev said. "He wants to talk to you. Says he has something you need and wants to give it to you."

"Did you ask him what it was?"

"I did," Bev said, "but he said he had to give it to you personally. Said he missed you earlier."

"Earlier?" Dix asked.

"That's what he said," Bev replied. "I called you as soon as I hung up on him."

"So you think he might have come by the office earlier?"

"I think so," Bev said.

Dix took a deep breath to calm his thinking. Suddenly there was yet another hope. "Did he leave an address or number to call?"

"Number," Bev said.

"Give it to me and I'll call him and set up a meeting. Gather everyone up and stand by. Be ready to move fast."

Bev gave him the number, Dix hung up and then dialed Brad Barringer's number.

"Yeah?" a man's voice said on the other end of the line.

"Brad Barringer, this is Dixon Hill."

"Yeah," the man said.

"I hear you've been lookin' for me."

"I sure have," Barringer said. "Been up to your office earlier and just talked to your secretary on the line. She sounded hot. Is she hot, Hill?"

Dix ignored his question. "I sure don't know how I missed you at my office." Dix kept his voice as low and level as he could make it, "When did you stop by?"

"Around five I would guess," Barringer said. "No one was in your office and two guys were working on a wall in the hallway. Wish the broad had been there."

"Maybe next time. Where can I meet you?"

"I'm tired of coming to your place," Barringer said, "you come by here."

"Where is here?" Dix asked.

Barringer gave him the address, a building about five blocks away.

"I'll stop by on my way back to my office," Dix said.

"Great," Barringer said, "I'll be expecting you."

With that the phone went dead in Dix's hand.

Dix quickly dialed his own office and told Bev to get everyone to a location outside of Barringer's apartment in five minutes. Then, at a run, he headed down the hallway to get Detective Bell.

Within one minute Bell had someone checking the evidence locker for the Heart, just in case it had been found in Andrews' apartment, and he and Dix were headed back out into the hard, cold rain.

Section Three: Breaking Laws

As they sped toward Brad Barringer's apartment in Detective Bell's big Dodge four door, the rain suddenly stopped and half a block later the stars were out and the sky clear.

"This night ever goin' ta end?" Bell asked as he slid the big Dodge into a four-wheeled slide over the wet pavement and around a corner, correcting the slide perfectly and roaring down the middle of the street, the acceleration pressing Dix back in his part of the front bench seat.

"If we find that golden ball it will," Dix said, holding on to the door handle and trying to focus ahead. "If not, this is the last night any of us will ever see."

"It would be nice to see another sunrise," Bell said as he bounced the car through an intersection without a thought of another car coming from either side. "And my wife and kids. How long do you think we have before this all goes away, or whatever is going to happen happens?"

"About an hour," Dix said. "Maybe less."

The words sort of hung in the car, covering even the roaring of the engine with the deadening reality.

Neither of them said anything as Bell slid the car to a stop a few hundred paces from Barringer's apartment building. From the other direction Dix could see Bev, Mr. Data, Whelan, and the others running toward them, spreading out, covering back entrances and the alley between the buildings.

Both Dix and Bell jumped out of the car and headed toward the address Barringer had given Dix.

"You know we're about to break about a hundred laws here," Bell said, not slowing even slightly as they ran up the sidewalk.

"Arrest me tomorrow," Dix said, "if there is a tomorrow."

"Couldn't do that," Bell said, "I'd have to arrest myself at the same time."

"Boss," Mr. Data said as he met them at the base of the steps leading up to Barringer's apartment. "We have the building surrounded."

Bev came to a stop beside Mr. Data, then leaned down and rubbed the tops of her feet. "If we get out of this, I'll never wear high heels again."

"Too bad," Bell said, winking at her, "they look good on ya."

"Yeah," Mr. Data said, looking down at the Luscious Bev's legs. "Nice gams. Great sticks. They go all the way to the ground. You couldn't—"

Dix held up his hand for Mr. Data to stop, then pulled his gun out and looked around the dark street. There were no lights on in any of the windows, including those in Barringer's building. "We go in quick and fast. Mr. Data, I want you to knock down his door."

"Understood," Mr. Data said.

Without another word Dix headed up the stairs, with Bell and Mr. Data behind him.

Two flights up, and down a fairly dark and damp corridor that smelled of urine, they found the address that Barringer had given him. With Bell on one side, gun drawn, and Dix on the other, gun heavy in his hand, Mr. Data stood in front of the door.

"Do it," Dix whispered.

Mr. Data raised his foot and kicked right next to the lock.

The door smashed inward, banging like a shot against the wall.

Mr. Data went in first, right at Barringer.

Dix ducked right, Bell left.

Barringer was caught completely by surprise, sitting at a small kitchen table, a spoonful of cereal halfway to his mouth. He was wearing a sweat-stained muscle shirt and his hair hadn't been combed in some time.

"What the—"

"You move, we'll shoot you and ask questions later," Bell said, moving at Barringer. He took the spoon out of Barringer's hand, forced the man to his feet, and quickly handcuffed his hands.

"You can't do this!" Barringer shouted. "I got rights!"

"You got rights to be dead," Detective Bell said, "and that's exactly what's going to happen if you don't take it easy and answer some questions."

"Mr. Data, get everyone up here," Dix said, glancing around at the three-room apartment filled with old furniture and stacks of movie and theater magazines. "We're going to need to search this place and do it quickly."

"For what?" Barringer asked as Detective Bell slammed him back into his chair and pushed it away from the table so he'd be easier to guard.

"For what you took out of the device sitting at the top of the stairs in my office," Dix said, moving toward Barringer. "Save us the time of tearing this place apart and tell me where it is."

"We take it, we leave, no harm done, I never report it," Bell said. "Seems fair enough to me."

Barringer stared at Dix, clearly confused. "I have no idea what you are talking about."

"A golden ball," Dix said, "that you took from the machine at the top of the stairs."

"There was no golden ball in that machine," Barringer said. "And I didn't take anything else either. I just paced around your office once and left."

Dix stared at Barringer. Was it possible this was yet another dead end? "So what did you want to give me?"

Bell nodded at a stack of letters on the end of the table. "Those."

"What are they?" Dix asked, picking them up and glancing at the envelopes. Almost instantly he answered his own question.

"Letters from Marci," Barringer said, "to me. In a couple of them she tells me she's worried about her husband killing her if he found out she was back seeing me. I figured they could help you put that slime husband of hers away for good."

Behind Dix the sound of his people coming up the stairs filled the hallways. Dix turned around as Bev came through the door first, followed by Mr. Data, Carter, Whelan, and the rest.

"Search this place," Dix said. "And quickly."

"Hey, I told you I didn't take your golden ball or whatever it was!" Barringer shouted.

Bell kicked the leg of Barringer's chair, jarring him.

"Calm down now and let these people do what they have to do," Bell said.

Without a question Dix's people spread out.

"You're making a mess!" Barringer said, his voice pathetic.

"I'll pay for a maid to come and clean," Dix said, "assuming you're telling me the truth."

"And fix my door."

"And fix the door," Dix said. "I promise."

But unless they found the Heart in this apartment, he doubted he was going to have to pay up on that promise, or any other for that matter.

Clues from Dixon Hill's notebook in "The Case of the Missing Heart"

- Detective Bell didn't make it to Dix's office around five.
- Arnie Andrews was there, but claimed he saw nothing. Nothing was found in his apartment.
- Brad Barringer was there during the time the Adjuster was unguarded.

Chapter Ten

The Obvious Ain't Always Obvious

Section One: Empty

DESPAIR FILLED THE AIR like thick humidity, pressing in on everything, wrapping around Dixon Hill's face and hands and body, making him want to just sit down. He pushed it away. There was still a little time yet. Some solution might yet be found.

Brad Barringer's apartment had turned up nothing in the way of a small golden-looking ball. And between Mr. Data and Bev and the rest of Dix's crew, they had touched and looked at everything. Mr. Data had even found a special hidden drawer where Barringer kept a bottle of special hair lotion, guaranteed to help him grow more and thicker hair. Mr. Data had told him it wouldn't work and Barringer had just shrugged.

"You goin' to pay for all this mess?" Barringer asked

as Bell uncuffed him from the chair and patted him on the shoulder.

Dix's people, except for Mr. Data and Bev, had all filed out and were waiting downstairs. Outside, it looked like it was still clear; the rain was holding off, at least on this block. Who knew what the weather might be like back at Dix's office.

"Looks just like it did when we came in, doesn't it, Dix?" Bell asked, pretending to look around the apartment and the mess they had just created.

"Yeah," Dix said, glancing around hoping for something they had missed. He picked up Marci's letters to Brad from the corner of the table. They smelled faintly of a woman's perfume. A light perfume, not like the stuff Jessica Daniels must have poured over her entire body.

He handed the letters to Detective Bell. "I just bet these are enough to put Andrews away for a very long time. You want to make sure the cops doing the case get them."

Dix wanted to add *If there is a tomorrow.* But he didn't.

Bell took the letters, glanced at the top envelope and slipped them into his coat pocket.

"Can I get those back some time?" Barringer asked, looking slightly panicked. "They're all I got left to remember her by."

Bell nodded. "Sure, you don't mention our little visit tonight and you'll get these back right after they slam the lockup on Andrews. Deal?"

Barringer frowned, then nodded. "Deal."

"Let's go," Dix said to Bev. He headed out into the urine-smelling hall. It seemed darker than when they had come up, but more than likely that was just his mood.

They had less than an hour until everything was destroyed.

An hour and no leads.

No real chance of finding that gold ball that would save this world, and all the rest of the world and the people he loved.

Outside he moved up to the group of his people waiting for him on the sidewalk. None of them were talking. They all knew what failure meant. They were all dealing with the coming destruction and death in their own way.

Bev, Mr. Data, and Detective Bell joined them. "What's next?" Bell asked.

Dix looked around at his people. He couldn't give up, not while there was even the slightest chance of finding that golden ball. It was their best and only hope, from everything he was being told.

"We go over it one more time," Dix said, making up his mind to move.

Dix turned to Bell. "Would you grill Andrews one more time, and make sure that the ball isn't in the evidence room, either in Andrews' things, or anything brought in from any of the boss arrests?"

"Good thinking," Bell said, heading for his car. "I'll call you if I have any luck."

"Immediately," Dix said.

Bell waved that he had heard and almost dove into his car. A moment later the big Dodge, spinning its tires on the wet pavement, turned and sped off downtown.

"Mr. Data," Dix said, "you and the rest except for Bev give Andrews' apartment one more going-over. Make sure there are no hidden safes or loose floorboards, then come back to my office as fast as you can."

"Gotcha, boss," Mr. Data said, turning and leading everyone down the street at a very fast walk.

"What are we going to do?" Bev asked.

"We're going back to my office," Dix said. "And see if there's anyone else who might have been on those stairs. Anyone we might have missed."

He turned the collar of his coat up to keep the cold wind that had just kicked up from blowing on his neck and headed down the sidewalk.

Their steps echoed in the forever night, bouncing off the buildings, dying in the alleys. The wind cut at them, trying to hold them back, but there was still time, so nothing was going to stop him now.

There had to be something he had missed. He was not willing to fail.

"Anyone else have an office, or live in your building?" Bev asked after twenty steps.

Dix glanced at her and at the worried and tired look on her face. Clearly she wasn't giving up hope yet either.

"No," Dix said. "The building is almost condemned. The two other offices on my floor have been boarded up for as long as I have been there, and the apartments on the two floors above are also empty and unsafe to even go into. Floors rotted out."

"So who owns the building?" Bev asked. "Maybe the owner decided to come by."

"I own it," Dix said. He had never told anyone before, but the records of Dixon Hill showed that he had taken the old, condemned building in trade for a fee on a case a few years ago. He had fixed up the staircase and the one office on the second floor and boarded up all the rest.

"Oh," Bev said. "There's no owner to come by."

"I'm afraid not," Dix said.

Silence again ruled their walk.

The fog swirled past overhead, brushing the tops of the buildings like a light hand polishing fine works of art. In the distance a ship's horn blew, mournful and sad, echoing its lost-sounding cry through the night.

Dix, his collar up around his neck, his gaze focused ahead and on the details of this mystery, walked on-ward.

Bev stayed with him, at his side. He felt comfort with her there.

The seconds ticked past.

It was almost over.

Dixon Hill was going to fail for the first time on his biggest and most important case. And he wasn't going to just fail himself, but every friend and sleeping person behind the windows in the buildings they walked past, and everyone beyond this city.

He had failed. And failure was not something Dixon Hill took lightly.

Again the ship's foghorn echoed through the still city, crying for the night to end.

In less than an hour, Dixon Hill knew the end would come.

Section Two: No More Suspects

It took Dix and Bev less than five minutes of hard walking through the cold night air to reach his office. On the way up, Dix stopped on the landing and stared up at the second floor, trying to imagine what someone would have thought coming around that corner and seeing the Adjuster and the golden Heart sitting there, with no one watching it.

What kind of person would then sneak up the stairs, take the gold ball, and leave?

Any thief would have sold it at once and the ball would have ended up with Redblock or Harvey Upstairs Benton or Benny the Banger. That hadn't happened, so it hadn't been a petty thief who had come up the stairs and run into the opportunity.

But then who?

Not Andrews, not Bell, not Barringer, it would seem. Dix was all out of suspects.

Yet someone had taken that golden ball from the Adjuster, thinking it was worth something.

"Who?"

"I wish I knew," Bev said, standing beside him on the landing and staring upward.

Dix at first didn't realize he had spoken the question aloud. "I wish you did, too."

She touched his arm and they turned and headed on up into the office. He took off his coat and hat, then picked up his appointment book, flipping to the day before, hoping that maybe someone had gotten the wrong day.

There were no appointments at all on the day before, or the day after.

He flipped the book back onto the desk and began pacing, back and forth, as Bev stood in front of the window looking out at the cold night and the street below.

"Anyone else you talked to in the Marci case?" Bev asked. "Someone at the theater who might have come to give you a lead?"

"No one," Dix said. "I hadn't gotten very far on that case when this problem came up. No one but Bell, Andrews, and Barringer even knew I was working it."

"Not working for a client?"

"No," Dix said. "I just liked her and her ability, so I thought I'd figure out who killed her."

Bev nodded and went back to silently staring out the window.

Dix paced, letting the movement clear his mind. He went over it all again, slowly, carefully, not letting the ticking seconds push him to miss anything.

But there just wasn't anything to miss.

"Do you think Redblock might have it in his pocket?" Bev asked, spinning around as the idea stuck her.

"No," Dix said. "Redblock was snatched by whoever did that hours before the Heart was taken from the hallway. He'd have no chance to have gotten it from one of his people."

Bev nodded and turned back to the window. In the reflection in the glass he could see the worry etched on her face. He wished he could comfort her, make it better, but at this point the only comfort they were going to get was in the shape of a small golden-looking ball.

Dix headed out through the front office again and stopped in the doorway, staring at where the Adjuster had been. The empty space on the floor shouted failure at him.

He glanced down the hall in both directions. Nothing, and no way out. Mr. Data and Mr. La Forge had been to the right, and to the left were only the other two offices boarded up around the corner.

Behind him the phone rang. He moved back into the outer office and picked it up as Bev joined him.

"Dix?" Bell's voice came clearly over the line.

"Any luck?" Dix asked.

"Nothing," Bell said. "I had six cops help me search every inch of the evidence room. Nothing gold and round has come in there in anything."

"Andrews?"

"They're cleaning him up and putting him back in his cell," Bell said. "Trust me, he didn't take it."

"Thanks," Dix said. "It was worth the shot."

"It was at that," Bell said. "What do you want me to do now?"

"Go home and crawl in bed with that wife of yours," Dix said. "Give her a hug for me. And if the sun comes up, celebrate."

"Will do," Bell said, his voice soft. "You call me if you need help."

"I will do that, my friend," Dix said.

With that Bell hung up.

Dix gently put the phone back in its cradle just as the sound of the door opening below filled the hallway and office. Dix knew it would be Mr. Data and the rest, coming back empty-handed as well.

He moved past Bev and back into his office. There he sat down in his chair and looked at the wooden surface of his desk. There had to be something.

There just had to be.

But they had just over thirty minutes of time left.

Through the open door Dix saw Mr. Whelan, Mr. Carter, and the others file in and spread out, some dropping into chairs, others just leaning against the wall. Mr. Data came in last holding Spot, his cat, scratching the cat's ears.

"No luck, boss," Mr. Data said. "The place was as clean as they come."

"No old sayings, Mr. Data," Dix asked.

"It did seem appropriate," he said.

"Where did you find Spot?" Bev asked.

"He must have gotten in here when the doors were

stuck open," Mr. Data said. "He was just in the hallway. He seems hungry and glad to see me."

Arnie Andrews' words came flowing back into Dix's mind.

"Nothing but some stray cat," Andrews had said when Dix asked him if there was anything in the hallway.

Spot!

There was *one* more suspect.

Spot!

Dix sprang out of his chair, knocking it over backward as he headed around his desk for the door.

"What?" Bev asked. "What are you thinking?"

Dix smiled. "Mr. Data, didn't Sherlock Holmes once say to Watson, 'The most difficult crime to track is the one that is purposeless.'?"

"He did, boss," Mr. Data said, *"In The Adventure of the Naval Treaty."*

"We've been assuming this theft of the golden Heart had a purpose," Dix said, laughing. "We thought someone took the Heart because it looked like it was valuable. That's where we went wrong. That was our false assumption."

"What else could it be?" Bev asked, staring at Dix.

Dix stopped in front of Mr. Data and scratched Spot's right ear, making the cat purr loudly.

"A toy," Dix said. "The Heart looked like a toy ball."

In both rooms everyone froze, silent. The sound of thinking had never had such energy.

Dix smiled and strode through the outer office and into the hallway.

"Spot?" Bev asked after a moment, running after him. "You think Spot took the Heart?"

"When all other options have been eliminated, the remaining option must be the truth," Dix said. "I heard that somewhere." He held up his hand for Mr. Data to stop giving him the exact reference and wording. They had work to do.

"So where would a cat, playing with a ball, take it?" Dix asked, looking both directions down the hallway, then down the stairs.

"Back to its home," Bev said as she and the others filed out into the hallway with him.

"Possible," Dix said. "Mr. Data, take Spot home and check anywhere Spot may have hidden a ball there. Have Mr. Riker start a full search as well of everything else, especially anything between here and there. Then, if you have no luck, come right back."

"Understood," Mr. Data said, heading quickly for the door, Spot still purring in his arms.

"Mr. Whelan, go get us a dozen flashlights."

"Will do, boss," Mr. Whelan said and followed Mr. Data out the door.

"Now, everyone else," Dix said, "spread out, starting on this floor and working down and out around the front steps. Be quick, but don't miss anything. Our lives depend on thinking like a cat right now."

"I didn't know that was possible," Bev said.

"We have thirty minutes to make it possible," Dix said.

Section Three: Where Oh Where Has Spot's Ball Gone?

It took Mr. Whelan just a minute to come back with the flashlights, but in that time they had scoured the hallway carefully, checking all the corners and working down the staircase, looking for anywhere a cat might have knocked a ball it was playing with.

Dix and Bev took two of the flashlights and went up to the next floor, stopping at the top. All the doors were boarded up and there was dust everywhere.

"Careful," Dix said, "the floors out here are still pretty solid, but step lightly and test your footing. I'll go right, you go left."

"Will do," Bev said.

Using the flashlight to sweep the edges of the hallway and all the cracks, he moved slowly down the hall. The boards creaked under his feet, but remained fairly solid. If Spot had brought the Heart up here to play with, it would be in plain sight. Everything else was boarded up tight, too tight for the Heart or a cat to fit through.

"Nothing this way," Bev said just after Dix had checked to make sure the window leading to the fire escape outside was still locked and boarded. That fire escape was more dangerous than the floor in the hall.

"Okay," Dix said, turning to meet Bev. "We go back down. Nothing up here. No hole big enough for the Heart to go through."

Bev nodded and headed down, shining the light

along the edges to make sure they hadn't missed anything on the way up.

"Anything?" Mr. Whelan asked as they met on the landing where the Adjuster had sat.

"Nothing up there," Dix said. "How about down here?"

"Only one possibility on this floor," Mr. Whelan said. He pointed with the beam of his flashlight down the hall toward the two boarded-up offices.

"Show me," Dix said.

Whelan led the way, but instead of turning toward the two other offices, he turned and pointed toward the end of a short part of the hall. There was a crack at the base of the wall and a board had been knocked aside at one point in the past, leaving a triangle-shaped hole big enough for the Heart of the Adjuster and Mr. Data's cat Spot to fit through.

"I tried to shine my light in there," Mr. Whelan said, "But I couldn't see anything. You might want to try."

Dix nodded and got down on his hands and knees and directed his light in through the hole, squinting to make out anything golden in there. The light was blocked by something that was about arm's-length inside the hole. Spot could easily have rolled the ball down the hall while playing with it, and knocked it in there, then sideways.

Dix stood and stepped back, staring at the dead end in the corridor. "I wonder what this used to be?"

"Maybe a walled-over dumbwaiter shaft," Bev said. "Or a closet? Or a service elevator."

"Or a regular elevator that someone in the past gave up on," Mr. Whelan said.

Dix nodded. All of that made sense. He shined his light over the wall. It clearly had been boarded up and patched to make it look like the other walls, but time had broken some of the plaster and warped a few of the boards to show where the fix had been made.

"I wonder why anyone would do that?" Mr. Whelan asked.

"I have no idea," Dix said, "There's nothing in the records of the building about anything here, but we need to get in there to make sure the Heart isn't back there."

"Mr. Data," Bev said, calling down the hall. "We're here. We could use your help."

Dix stepped back so that he could see down the hall-way as Mr. Data, without Spot, walked toward them. "Any luck?"

"No, boss," Mr. Data said. "But the search is continuing."

Dix pointed at the walled-over end of the short corridor. "Can you pull enough of those boards off so we can see and get in there?"

"I can," Mr. Data said.

He moved forward and then, his fingers pointed, jammed his hand into the wall, sending plaster dust and wood flying.

Bev coughed and stepped back as Mr. Data pulled on the board, ripping it free and setting it aside.

Then he pulled on the next one and the next one,

until there was an opening in the wall large enough for a man to step easily through.

Dix, his flashlight in hand, moved up through the plaster dust and stuck his head inside the wall. What greeted him wasn't at all what he expected.

The space was small, no more than two steps deep. On the back wall were some coat hooks. This had been an old closet, that was clear.

And sitting on the floor, his back against the wall, was the skeleton of a man wearing a black suit and a black hat and matching black shoes.

"Fascinating," Dix said, shining his light over the skeleton. The white of the skull seemed to glow and grin at Dix, like an actor in the spotlight.

"It seems that if we find the Heart, I might have a new case," Dix said.

"What?" Bev asked.

Dix backed up a moment to let Bev and Mr. Data glance through the opening, then he went back, crouching down so he could shine his light easier through the dust and search the floor area of the hole.

Around the skeleton's chest hung what looked like a sign, but it was so covered in dust, Dix couldn't read it. Clearly this body had been here a very, very long time.

He shone the light along the base of the left side wall, then the back wall, and finally along the skeleton's old suit, looking for anyplace a cat might have shoved a ball.

Something glinted near the skeleton's knee, just under the edge of his pants.

Dix reached in and pulled up the old cloth. It came apart in his hand, exposing bone.

Beside the skeleton's upper leg bone was a golden ball.

The Heart of the Adjuster!

"Found it!" Dix shouted.

The cheer behind him sounded like a much larger crowd than the few people helping him.

Dix eased through the hole Mr. Data had created and picked up the Heart, then eased back and stood. He held the Heart of the Adjuster up for everyone to see, shining his light on it.

Then he handed it to Mr. Data.

"Oh, thank heaven," Bev said, the weariness in her voice very clear.

"We found it!" Whelan shouted, then ran to the stairs and called down to the others still searching. "We found it!"

"Get this in the Adjuster and get it working," Dix said to Mr. Data. "Quickly. There can't be much time left."

Mr. Data held up the Heart. "So this is what a McGuffin looks like."

He turned with the golden ball and trotted down the hallway toward the doorway. It was one of the first times Dix had seen Mr. Data run.

"So Spot really was our criminal," Bev said, leaning against the wall. The dust and the relief on her face made her seem pale and weak, far from what Dix knew she really was.

"Amazing," Mr. Whelan said. "You really are a great detective."

Dix laughed and pointed his light into the hole. "It seems I solve one case and another appears out of the wall."

"What are you talking about?" Mr. Whelan asked.

"Take a look in there," Bev said, gesturing toward the torn-up wall.

Mr. Whelan moved past her and shone his flashlight in the hole. "A skeleton behind a wall? Isn't that an old idea?"

Mr. Whelan then stepped through the hole and eased the sign off the skeleton's neck. He came back out, blowing lightly on the dust covering the sign, sending swirls of particles through the flashlight beams.

"What does it say?" Dix asked, shining his light on the rudely cut piece of cardboard.

"I think," Bev said, leaning over Mr. Whelan's shoulder and studying the lettering, "it mentions your name."

"What?" Dix asked.

Whelan shook the sign, then Bev carefully brushed off the last of the dust with her sleeve.

Then she read, " 'Hah, hah, Dixon Hill. Next time this will be you.' "

"It seems you have an enemy out there from a long time ago," Bev said.

"After tonight," Dix said, "I think that's the least of my worries. Let's go see if the Adjuster is working. This case can wait just a little longer. Not going to hurt that guy."

He took Bev by the arm and they headed for the door.

As always, it felt good to solve a case.

Clues from Dixon Hill's notebook in "The Case of the Missing Heart"

- Case solved. The Heart of the Adjuster recovered. Spot, the cat, was the bad guy.
- However, there is a skeleton in the wall of my building, with a sign on it threatening me.
- Cyrus Redblock is still missing.

Chapter Eleven

A Big Loose End

*Twenty-four hours after
the Heart of the Adjuster was found*

Captain's Log.
The Enterprise *is slowly backing away from the*
Blackness. *Little did I know that when I left the*
holodeck, our problems would be far from over.

The first few minutes after finding the ball of
Auriferite, what we had been referring to as the Heart
of the Adjuster, Mr. Data and Chief Engineer La Forge
had the Adjuster working, focusing on blocking the
chaotic waves coming off the four quantum
singularities that formed the Blackness.

The Adjuster worked as their tests on the holodeck
had shown it would, before the Heart was used as a cat
toy. This allowed them to do an emergency restart of
the impulse engine.

The restart was successful, but the Enterprise *was so*

close at that point to the edge of the Blackness, that the thrusters had to be pushed to maximum within seconds to stop us in time.

The Adjuster, blocking 99.9 percent of the effects of the Blackness, still allowed some of the chaotic subspace waves through, and Engineer La Forge informs me that one such leakage caused the impulse engine to fail just moments after we stopped our forward momentum and reversed course. We started away from the terminal edge of the Blackness only two minutes from our sure destruction.

However, it then became a race against time to repair the impulse engines and again restart them as our momentum away from the Blackness was slowed and then stopped by the gravitational forces at play from the four quantum singularities.

Again, the clock was ticking. Fourteen hours was the calculation of the time until we were pulled across that deadly line and into the area of no return. The first restart of the impulse engines had bought us fourteen hours.

Six long hours after we escaped death the first time, our outward momentum stopped and we started drifting back toward the Blackness, slowly at first, but gaining speed with every passing moment.

I must commend the work of Chief Engineer La Forge and Mr. Data. They again, after seven hours of the impulse engines' failure, managed to get the impulse engines working, and this time to bring them up to power slowly, stopping the ship over a thirty-

minute period, and then moving it away with ever-
increasing speed.

Mr. Data now assures me that even if the impulse
engines were to fail again, our speed and momentum
would carry us out of the effect area of the Blackness.
At that point we would be able to restart both the
warp drive and the impulse engines. I will not be
relieved, or satisfied, until we are a great distance
from this area.

> Three days, six hours after
> the Heart of the Adjuster was recovered

Captain's Log. Personal.
Chief Engineer La Forge informed me that the
moment we crossed out of the effects of the Blackness,
all standard features of the Dixon Hill program were
automatically reset, and all safety features were back in
place again. The program then shut down.

It has taken days of hard work to repair the ship
from all the damage caused by the brush with the
Blackness, and I am now again beginning to feel
rested, only just barely.

At some point I know I must face the world of the city
by the bay again. I am having difficulty accepting the
fact that the world that I use as relaxation almost cost
every life onboard this ship.

I mentioned this to Dr. Crusher, who actually
laughed. She said it was that world, and Dixon Hill's
ability to see that world, that saved us. She said that

Spot could have easily ended up playing with the Heart of the Adjuster in a jungle climate and we never would have found it.

I agreed that she had a point.

She told me we were lucky that the holodeck, when it malfunctioned, went back to the most recent program it had been running, and that I knew that program.

I understand her thinking, but I still think I will wait at least a few more days, maybe a week, until I return to that world.

Section One: When Is a Game a Game? And a Toy a Toy?

It had been almost two weeks since Dixon Hill had been in his office. Outside the window the streets were filled with people going about their normal daily activities. Cars swished by on the street, splashing the puddles left from a recent shower like so many kids on their way home from school.

Dix stood at the window in his second-floor office, watching the normal traffic, listening to the sounds of the distant ship's horns. There was just something about this place, this city, that he loved. And he figured it was his imagination, but the city also felt better now, as if cleaned and washed and hung out in the wonderful weather to dry.

Imagination or not, it was a wonderful feeling.

He pushed open the big, wooden-framed window, letting in the sounds as if turning up the volume of a radio. The fresh air swirled around him with the street noise, bringing the reality of the city inside, hugging him, pulling him outward, as if a beautiful woman calling him to her bed.

He would go out there soon enough.

He took another deep breath of the fresh ocean air, then turned back to his desk. First he had some questions that needed answers.

He picked up the phone from its cradle and by memory dialed the short number for the downtown police precinct.

Detective Bell, as always, was busy. And it took a few minutes for him to come to the phone from the interrogation room, where no doubt he had been sweating the confession out of some robber or murderer.

"Hey, Dix," Bell said, "glad to hear you're back from vacation."

"Glad to be back," Dix said, understanding suddenly that time had passed in this city as well as outside the city.

"So what's the honor?" Bell asked. "You in trouble again? Wrong woman chasing you?"

"Not yet," Dix said, laughing. "But I do have two quick questions that might sound stupid."

"Dix," Bell said, "if a friend can't laugh at you, who can? Ask away."

"Is Cyrus Redblock still in charge of the city?"

Bell laughed as promised. "You're right, stupid question. Of course he is. No one would be crazy enough to challenge him. What makes you think anyone would? You got information I don't have? Come on, spill it."

"Nothing," Dix said. "I just had a dream about Redblock losing control."

"Nightmare would be more like it," Bell said. "You sure don't want any of the smaller crime bosses taking over."

"You can say that again. How about the Marci Andrews killing? Anyone arrested for that?"

"Her husband is in jail," Bell said. "They arrested him yesterday when some guy gave us letters she wrote saying she was afraid of her husband killing her. From what I understand, they found a gun with her blood splattered on it hidden in his car. Open and shut case."

"Well," Dix said, "I guess that case is solved."

"Completely," Bell said. "Got to run. Got a guy under the light sweatin' like a leaky fire hose. How about dinner soon with you and the Luscious Bev and me and the wife?"

"You got it," Dix said.

"Great," Bell said, and hung up.

Dix put the phone back in its cradle and took another deep breath of the wonderful fresh air.

The world had reset.

Or at least the criminal part of it, which relieved Dix. Dealing with Redblock was bad enough, but dealing with Harvey Upstairs Benton, a used car salesman given too much power, scared Dix more than he wanted to admit.

He moved to the window. The fresh air and the street sounds were like a comforting concert of smells and noise, all mixing to ease his tension. This world, this city by the bay, hadn't been to blame for the loss of the Heart of the Adjuster. That had been just bad luck.

And the playfulness of a cat using the wrong toy at the wrong time.

"Okay, one more question to answer," Dix said to the empty room and the active street below. "Just one more and I can get on to the next case, whatever that's going to be."

He turned and headed out through his outer office and into the hallway. There he turned left and went down the hall to the small area that had been boarded off.

The wall was again smooth, with only the loose board near the floor where Spot had crawled inside playing with the Heart of the Adjuster. Even the physical parts of this world had reset after the night that seemed like it would never end. And in re-setting, the wall had been put back as it was before Mr. Data had ripped it down and filled the hallway with dust.

But the question was, had the skeleton been there before the changes? Or was it part of the craziness of that long night?

"Boss?" Mr. Data called out from inside the office. He had asked permission to join Dix when he went back to work, and Dix had gladly said yes. The

Luscious Bev would also be joining them any moment.

"Out here, Mr. Data," Dix said.

Mr. Data, dressed in the same suit that had smelled so bad before but now seemed fresh and well-pressed, stepped into the hallway and came toward him.

"It has been reset," Dix said, pointing to the wall as Mr. Data neared.

"Logical, boss," Mr. Data said.

"You still think there's a skeleton back there?" Bev asked as she came out of the office and moved down the hall to join them.

She looked even more stunning than Dix could ever remember. She had on a tight dress, a stole, and a wide-brimmed hat that gave her a hidden and mysterious look.

"I honestly don't know," Dix said. "But the hole in the wall is still there."

Bev touched Dix on the shoulder, smiled at him without taking her gaze from his eyes. It was a promise of much, much more, and considering how she looked tonight, he liked that promise.

After a moment she broke away and looked at the hole in the base of the wall. "I am still amazed you found the Heart, especially in a place like this."

Mr. Data took his gangster stance. "As Dexter Drake said, 'The solving of almost every crime mystery depends on something which seems, at first glance, to bear no relation whatever to the original crime.'"

"Well put," Dix said. "I could not agree more. This was just luck."

"It was more than luck," Bev said, stroking his arm. "It was the ability to see Spot in Mr. Data's arms, link it with information from a witness earlier, and come to a logical conclusion. Detective work at its best."

"Well, thank you," Dix said, smiling back at her. "But we still don't know who the skeleton belonged to, and how it got back there, or if it is even still back there."

"The classic loose end," Mr. Data said. "It must always be tied up at the end of a story. I can give you a list of a hundred loose ends, for example, in the story—"

"No, thank you, Mr. Data," Dix said, stopping his friend. "I think the one we have is more than enough."

"I suppose there is only one way to find out if there really is a loose end here," Bev said.

"Mr. Data," Dix said, nodding at the wall, "would you do the honors?"

"With pleasure, I'm sure," Mr. Data said, stepping up to the wall. "Besides, it was Felix Norman who said, 'No man is qualified to remove the skeleton from his own closet.' "

Dix and Bev both laughed.

"I think that was meant in a different fashion," Bev said.

Mr. Data looked at her, clearly puzzled.

"I'll explain it later," Dix said. "Now to the task at hand."

Mr. Data nodded and turned to the wall. "I will attempt to raise less dust this time."

"Thank you," Bev said as she and Dix both stepped back into the main hallway.

Carefully, Mr. Data pulled boards and plaster from an area of the wall, setting them to one side. There was still some dust floating in the air like steam in a steam bath, but not as bad as the last time. However, Mr. Data's clean black suit soon became pale as the dust covered it like bees to honey.

As Mr. Data finished, Dix took a flashlight from his pocket. He had brought it for this very purpose. Without stepping closer to keep from getting covered with dirt, he turned it on. The beam cut through the dust like a searchlight in the night sky, searching until it found its target inside the wall.

The skeleton, dressed in a fancy black suit and black hat, stared back at them from the opening, its eyes empty, dark holes staring from some unseen past.

The sign was still tied around its neck and lying on its chest.

"It seems this loose end just got longer and looser," Bev said, touching Dix's arm.

Mr. Data stepped through the hole he had made and took the cardboard sign off the skeleton, then moved back out into the hallway and handed it to Dix.

Dix shook the sign, then gently blew the dust off,

sending particles swirling through the beam of the flashlight and around the head of the skeleton like a million tiny flies.

The words on the sign seemed to jump off at him.

Hah, hah, Dixon Hill. Next time this will be you.

"Wow, you do make enemies," Bev said, laughing.

Dix stared at the sign, then moved over to the hole, ignoring the dirt, and shone his light on the skeleton in the boarded-up closet. "Bev, how long do you think this skeleton has been here? I'm guessing at least ten years, since this wall was like this before I bought the building."

"Ten at least," Bev said. "I'd guess more like fifteen. So what was Dixon Hill doing fifteen years ago?"

Dix laughed. "You know, I honestly don't remember. I'll have to go check."

"Shame on you," Bev said, lightly hitting his arm, "forgetting your own past."

"Easy to do," Dix said, winking at her, "when you live in the present."

He looked at the sign again, and this time two words popped off at him. *Next time.*

He pointed the two words out to Bev and Mr. Data. "I wonder what happened the first time?"

"This person was killed," Mr. Data said, "and put in here for you to find. That would suggest, using logical deduction, that you are destined to be killed and your body walled up, to be found years later by a cat playing with a ball."

Dix stared at his friend and then laughed along with

Bev. "Mr. Data, I'll leave the sayings up to you, you leave the deduction up to me."

Mr. Data frowned. "Of course, boss."

> *Sixteen days, eleven hours after the Heart of the Adjuster was retrieved*

Captain's Log. Personal.

I have again discovered the relaxation of the holodeck and the Dixon Hill program. The case that faces me is interesting, to say the least. Any time a skeleton is discovered locked into a wall, there are always mysteries afoot. And when that skeleton has a sign on its neck mentioning Dixon Hill, I am hooked into the case.

I have again recruited the help of Dr. Crusher and Mr. Data and Mr. Whelan in tracking down and finding who killed the man in the wall, and why. They have agreed, and each evening on our off duty time, we have decided to return to the city by the bay.

Granted, the feelings of the time spent in there searching for the Heart of the Adjuster come up at times, yet I feel the advantage of programs such as this one far outweigh the dangers and problems.

I have also filed a report with Starfleet, suggesting that another fail-safe be added to the holodecks. There needs to be some safety feature that saves anything brought into the holodeck from the outside when the holodeck is shut down. It has that fail-safe for humans and their clothes; it should be able to distinguish between matter brought in and matter created in the holodeck.

That simple safety procedure would never allow the loss of something important in a holodeck again.

But for now, Dixon Hill has a very important mystery to solve. A skeleton boarded up in a wall fifteen years ago wears a threat against him. I must discover what Dixon Hill was doing fifteen years ago, long before I walked into that world.

Somewhere in Dixon Hill's past there is an answer. It's just going to take time to find. And luckily, this time, Dixon Hill and his friends have the time.

Section Two: An Old Crime, A New Case

It was raining in the city by the bay, the drops were pounding the pavement, wearing at it before flowing into the gutters and sewers.

Dixon Hill glanced around at the empty street, the cars parked along the sidewalk, the mostly dark windows of apartments. Then he stepped down into the street and pulled his collar up around his neck, blocking some of the pelting drops from reaching his jacket and shirt. The fog drifted in over the tops of the buildings, letting the lights from the street corners bounce back with the rain, clearly lighting his way.

In the distance a ship's foghorn wailed, sending its sad-sounding cry echoing over the city. The smell of the docks was strong tonight, thick with fish and seaweed and salt. A familiar smell, like the scent of a mother to a child.

The click of his heels on the pavement was like the beat of a heart, sometimes lost in the rain, other times clear, constantly there with him. Dixon Hill took a deep breath of the night air and stared ahead through the rain, always watching where he was headed.

Somewhere out there, in this city by the bay, was a murderer. And he would not rest until the case was solved. And tonight he had a lead. Not much of one, but a lead.

Which might turn into a better clue, and then more and more clues, until finally the murderer of the man in the wall sat in jail where he belonged.

Again the ship's foghorn echoed over the buildings.

Dixon Hill was on the case.

Around him the city slept, peacefully resting for another day.

It was raining in the city by the bay. A hard rain.

Clues from Dixon Hill's notebook in "The Case of the Man in the Wall"

- The man has been in there for at least fifteen years.
- Someone killed him to threaten Dixon Hill.
- But if the man was killed as a threat, why was the body boarded up behind a wall that might never be opened?

- All this is a loose end from another case and it might never be tied up. Sometimes it is just better to let skeletons from a person's past stay in the closet.

(Author's note: "The Case of the Man in the Wall" remains to this day Dixon Hill's only unsolved mystery.)

Look for STAR TREK fiction from Pocket Books

Star Trek®: The Original Series

Star Trek: Deep Space Nine®

#17 • *The Heart of the Warrior* • John Gregory Betancourt
#18 • *Saratoga* • Michael Jan Friedman
#19 • *The Tempest* • Susan Wright
#20 • *Wrath of the Prophets* • David, Friedman & Greenberger
#21 • *Trial by Error* • Mark Garland
#22 • *Vengeance* • Dafydd ab Hugh
#23 • *The 34th Rule* • Armin Shimerman & David R. George III
#24-26 • *Rebels* • Dafydd ab Hugh
    #24 • *The Conquered*
    #25 • *The Courageous*
    #26 • *The Liberated*

Books set after the Series
    The Lives of Dax • Marco Palmieri, ed.
    Millennium • Judith and Garfield Reeves-Stevens
        #1 • *The Fan of Terok Nor*
        #2 • *The War of the Prophets*
        #3 • *Inferno*
A Stitch in Time • Andrew J. Robinson
Avatar, Book One • S.D. Perry
Avatar, Book Two • S.D. Perry
Section 31: Abyss: • David Weddle & Jeffrey Lang
Gateways #4: Demons of Air and Darkness • Keith R.A. DeCandido
Gateways #7: What Lay Beyond: "Horn and Ivory" • Keith R.A. DeCandido

Star Trek: Voyager®

Mosaic • Jeri Taylor
Pathways • Jeri Taylor
Captain Proton: Defender of the Earth • D.W. "Prof" Smith
Novelizations
    Caretaker • L.A. Graf
    Flashback • Diane Carey
    Day of Honor • Michael Jan Friedman
    Equinox • Diane Carey
    Endgame • Diane Carey & Christie Golden

#1 • *Caretaker* • L.A. Graf
#2 • *The Escape* • Dean Wesley Smith & Kristine Kathryn Rusch
#3 • *Ragnarok* • Nathan Archer
#4 • *Violations* • Susan Wright
#5 • *Incident at Arbuk* • John Gregory Betancourt
#6 • *The Murdered Sun* • Christie Golden
#7 • *Ghost of a Chance* • Mark A. Garland & Charles G. McGraw
#8 • *Cybersong* • S.N. Lewitt

Enterprise™

Star Trek®: New Frontier

Star Trek®: Starfleet Corps of Engineers (eBooks)

Star Trek®: Section 31™

Rogue • Andy Mangels & Michael A. Martin
Shadow • Dean Wesley Smith & Kristine Kathryn Rusch
Cloak • S. D. Perry
Abyss • Dean Weddle & Jeffrey Lang

Star Trek®: Gateways

#1 • *One Small Step* • Susan Wright
#2 • *Chainmail* • Diane Carey
#3 • *Doors Into Chaos* • Robert Greenberger
#4 • *Demons of Air and Darkness* • Keith R.A. DeCandido
#5 • *No Man's Land* • Christie Golden
#6 • *Cold Wars* • Peter David
#7 • *What Lay Beyond* • various

Star Trek®: The Badlands

#1 • Susan Wright
#2 • Susan Wright

Star Trek®: Dark Passions

#1 • Susan Wright
#2 • Susan Wright

Star Trek® Omnibus Editions

Invasion! Omnibus • various
Day of Honor Omnibus • various
The Captain's Table Omnibus • various
Star Trek: Odyssey • William Shatner with Judith and Garfield Reeves-Stevens
Millennium Omnibus • Judith and Garfield Reeves-Stevens
Starfleet: Year One • Michael Jan Friedman

Other Star Trek® Fiction

Legends of the Ferengi • Ira Steven Behr & Robert Hewitt Wolfe
Strange New Worlds, vols. I, II, III, and IV • Dean Wesley Smith, ed.
Adventures in Time and Space • Mary P. Taylor
Captain Proton: Defender of the Earth • D.W. "Prof" Smith
New Worlds, New Civilizations • Michael Jan Friedman
The Lives of Dax • Marco Palmieri, ed.
The Klingon Hamlet • Wil'yam Shex'pir
Enterprise Logs • Carol Greenburg, ed.
Amazing Stories Anthology • various